Royal Spring

R.G. Lindsey

ROYAL SPRING

ISBN 0-9735272-9-3

Legal deposit: The National Library of Canada, 2004

Cover design by Data Resolutions, Montreal
Printed in Canada by Data Resolutions, Montreal, Quebec

Cover photo: Soldiers strolling with girl friends, Toronto
(circa 1915) City of Toronto Archives, Fonds 1244 Item 137

Dedicated to my wife Wilma,
our sons and daughters and their spouses
and our grandchildren

*...look to the rock from which you were hewn
and to the quarry from which you were digged...*

Gratitude

Thanks to Mary Elizabeth Lindsey and Tamara Wilen-Kure for typing my handwritten manuscript into the computer, correcting grammatical errors, and making editorial suggestions; to Diana Fancher of the West Toronto Junction Historical Society who made helpful corrections; and to Eric Robinson and Evelyn Adam for their encouragement in this retirement venture.

Author's Note

Ontario's Humber and Don rivers (not to be confused with the much larger Humber and Don rivers found elsewhere) rise north of Toronto to flow south through undulating farmlands, wind through Metropolitan Toronto, and empty into Lake Ontario. Time was when both rivers provided power for many small communities like the 'Humber Bend' of Royal Spring. In the late Nineteenth and early Twentieth Centuries, an era that absorbs much of this novel, the Humber and Don had dwindling fish populations, powered numerous small grist and saw mills, and provided shady stretches in summer for boys to skinny dip.

In those days the sun hadn't set on the British Empire. Most communities, large and small, recruited militia units in accordance with the Militia Act. Attachment to King and Country, like cleanliness, was next to godliness, and the militia was one unquestioned expression of this belief.

In Royal Spring John Alexander Tyrone from Humber Bend moves to West Toronto Junction and goes into the Toronto Regiment (militia) as a matter of course. When war starts with Germany in August 1914 he 'goes active' with the regiment and is at the Second Battle of Ypres in April, 1915.

In 1936 the Toronto Regiment and the 10th Royal Grenadiers amalgamated to form the Royal Regiment of Canada. In the novel Tyrone's son, Roddy, enlists in the Royals at the outbreak of the Second World War in 1939. The regiment was decimated in the Dieppe Raid of August 19, 1942, but regrouped in England to go on and play a decisive role in the Normandy Campaign of 1944.

The regimental historian, Major W. R. Bennett CD, himself a survivor of Normandy, has this to say about the Dieppe Raid, "Callous political stupidity, supported by the folly of eager military leaders, guaranteed the catastrophe that was Dieppe from the very beginning. In 1854 Lord Cardigan's 'Charge of the Light Brigade' at Balaclava in the Crimean war and again in 1863, Pickett's notorious charge at Gettysburg in the American Civil War, both had far more hope of success than the Canadians at Dieppe. Unforgivable." (Dieppe Raid Casualties, revised 1990)

This is a work of fiction. All of the plot's main characters are fictitious, but I hope plausible and representative of their age and background. Throughout the story mention is made of some events and some persons that helped shape the age and give it colour; these are historically verifiable. But Siding Street and Royal Spring and Axle Company are inventions. I hope they represent something typical. Otherwise readers will find streets and places mentioned in the novel in current Toronto street maps and local histories, particularly West Toronto Junction Revisited (West Toronto Junction Historical Society, 1986).

– 1892 –

When John Alexander Tyrone came screaming into the world his parents were deeply relieved and grateful to God for he was both robust and without defect. Dr. Reddy's words added to their pleasure. "Congratulations! This boy will grow to lift a hundred weight like a feather."

William Tyrone had been a widower for eleven years when he married Joanna Strabane in 1891. Now, on February 21, 1892, his teenage children were below in the kitchen and heard the doctor's prophecy through the heating grill to the hall above. Amy, at fifteen, was learning millinery with Hattie Longford on Main Street. Watt, named after his mother's family, already showed some promise as an heir and at twelve helped after school and in the summer holidays at the mill.

The Tyrones, with their large farm on the outskirts of the village and their grist mill in Humber Bend itself and the Strabanes with their hardware, furniture making and undertaking business, were the most affluent and influential families in the community.

There would always be a Strabane or a Tyrone on the cemetery board, the school board, and as warden in the

Anglican church. Strabanes and Tyrones were listened to with respect in both the Orange and Masonic Lodges. The Strabane and Tyrone women frequently held office in the Anglican Women's Guild, the Imperial Order of the Daughters of the Empire and the Women's Christian Temperance Union. The Conservative members of the federal and provincial parliaments took care to cultivate the good will of the Strabanes and Tyrones. All in all, the Strabanes and Tyrones were people of social and economic substance.

The families had been related in Ireland and each sent branches to Upper Canada in 1830 to take up the offer of crown land grants. With lesser status than the colonial squirocracy, the Family Compact people, or of the United Empire Loyalists, they could nevertheless be valued as among the British faithful. Their credo was limited, but held with tenacity: family, Queen, Church, sobriety, sound management.

That evening, when Dr. Reddy was gone, the young Tyrones were brought in to see baby John. Then, as custom and necessity dictated, Mrs. Minty remained to spend the night with Joanna and the baby while the father, having dampened the draft in the box heater, stretched out for the night on the parlour couch. Mrs. Minty was already past middle age and before Dr. Reddy's arrival in the Eighties had for a decade been the local midwife. She herself was still raising a big family supported by her husband's paid labour in the Tyrone mill. Her qualification for the responsibility of midwife came through her own experiences of birthing and as assistant to Miss McCann the pioneer midwife in Humber Bend.

It was Mrs. Minty's conviction that there was no higher calling in this world than that of bringing babies into the light of day, particularly Protestant and Anglican babies, among whom none could be better suited to her standards than a Tyrone. She relished all the rituals surrounding a time of birth and from the first indications of a pregnancy until the day of Christening she could hardly contain her elation at this progression among the elect. As for Dr. Reddy, she deferred to his superior knowledge, but disdained his technique and seeming unawareness of the mighty work in which he was involved without as much as a breath of audible prayer before, during or after delivery. "Dear Jesus, there is no soul about some who do the Lord's work," she told her neighbour and primary confidant Mrs. Warminster. "He may be Dr. Reddy to some, but he's Dr. Rough 'n Reddy to me and it's a mercy that I'm on hand for these great moments that the good doctor hardly understands."

Mrs. Minty moved about the natal room as one with a purpose and a mission. The lamp was trimmed and lit; the baby was swabbed and placed in his cradle. Joanna's bed linen was changed and after being carefully sponged by Mrs. Minty she was helped into a fresh night dress. Then, when the entire scene was set — some hours before the baby would start to suckle — when all was accomplished (as the Bible might put it), then Mrs. Minty settled into the rocker by the lamp and intoned:

> *For everything there is a season, and a time for*
> *every matter under heaven:*
> *a time to be born, and a time to die,*
> *a time to plant, and a time to pluck*
> *up what is planted....*

"Mrs. Minty," broke in Joanna, "I'd like to sleep now. I'm very tired. Watch the baby and lift him to me when he is ready."

If it ever occurred to Joanna that a Tyrone would want a larger life than that provided by Humber Bend, she never gave voice to it. She was content with her lot as the young wife of the miller. Through all her life, she had a sense of the rightness and fitness of things about her and she could barely imagine them being ordered any differently. She loved the elm-lined streets and the Humber River itself coiling through town and the fragrances one found in Torrance's Dry Goods and General Store: fragrances that were a blend of calico, and tea, and old oiled floors; the scent of cedar hedges after a summer rain; the aroma passing out of kitchens where bread was being baked or fruits and vegetables preserved. The pungent smell of crushed grain from the dusty mill; the aroma of earth and newly mown hay and barns, filled her with pleasure. It seemed to her that even the buildings of Humber Bend were all part of a whole, intended to give satisfaction... MacSpadden's Blacksmith Shop, Joyce's Creamery, the Prince Hotel, the bandstand and the main street with its shady verandas.

Joanna was a favourite in the village, admired for her bearing, her spritely step, her fine features and bright brown eyes. Her response of laughter or of puckered brows to the gossip of Main Street was an almost daily feature of life in the village and over time came to indicate the limits of the acceptable, as though she was the undeclared but acknowledged doyenne of village etiquette. While she had had a number of suitors, including the young and eligible Presbyterian minister, the Reverend Johnston Blair, none fully engaged her affections until the widower Tyrone made his overtures in the winter and spring of 1889-1890 spanning a number of engagements that included a sugaring party at Watt's Maple Bush and the Methodist Ladies' Daffodil Tea. It was at the door of the Strabane residence on Queen Street that Tyrone asked her to let him request permission of Isaac Strabane for her hand.

The marriage in May of 1891 was before the full congregation of the Anglican church with some of those who couldn't gain entrance craning to see through the side windows, while others stood under the trees in the yard. They came out of the church in a rush, got into the Tyrone buggy and dashed for the station to get the 4:10 for Guelph with the full town in pursuit to wave them off at the station.

Now, some months later, after her visits to the stores on Main Street had declined by degrees, Joanna had fulfilled a dream of some years by giving birth to the infant John Alexander.

William and Joanna Tyrone were a couple who could rightly be described as steady and predictable, people of a fixed routine, rising at five throughout the year. The working day started at seven in the mill and continued until six in the evening, excepting Sundays, from April to November. Even through the months when the mill was idle, they rigorously maintained their early rising. With the mill in operation, there was a constant traffic of farmers' wagons, hayracks and buggies bringing grain into the mill and forming up under the shute beneath the grinding room to catch the 'chop' and then with a click-click of the tongue and a 'gid up there' head for home and the labours of farm life.

The Tyrones' religion rested more on the moral axioms

and forms of their Anglicanism than on the metaphysical. They respected the Mintys and other evangelicals in the village, but always found themselves uncomfortable when religious talk became personal or ardent. Only a very rare event, such as the fire in the mill's storehouse on the second Sunday of Advent in 1893, could keep the Tyrones home from church of a Sunday. The entire village knew that they could set their clocks by the appearance of Mr. and Mrs. Tyrone turning into the church drive shed behind Dolly and Prince who had been groomed to a glow by Fred, the yard man.

From his earliest days, John Alexander had had impressed upon him the significance and importance of time and routine. There was a time to rise, a time for breakfast, a time for an afternoon sleep, a time for supper, a time for prayers and a time for bed. It was a childhood regimen that fitted him superbly for both his soldiering days and business career as a man.

Like Joanna, John Alexander had a sense in his childhood that everything in Humber Bend was as the Almighty had intended and ordained. After he left Humber Bend, he never regained that sense of the fitness of things, and years after, in the soggy, rat infested trenches of the Ypres Salient, when the guns fell silent for a bit, he would think back as often as not to the time when he was six or seven and in the heat of the summer and allowed to sit out on the porch overlooking the mill pond. There, in the stillness, with no one making the effort to do anything other than savour the night with the occasional galumph of a tumescent bullfrog, he could hear the murmur of the stream as it spilled down into the mill race and feel as though he and his parents were at one with all that surrounded them. It never occurred to him then that any other reality could ever exist. At such times, Joanna would frequently, almost inaudibly, repeat the lines from the grade school reader, "God's in his heaven. All's right with the world."

When he reluctantly went up to bed, he would lay on the top of his feather tick in his little room under the eaves and there, drift into sleep thinking how fine Mr. Tracy McKibbon looked riding his tall chestnut mare and how someday he himself would be similarly mounted and trotting by on the road to Jefferson's bridge before the admiring eyes of his mother and sisters.

It fell to Joanna to watch over the development of young John Alex. She herself was content in the little world of Humber Bend, yet possibly as a consequence of her omnivorous reading she pictured John Alex' future unfolding on a larger stage.

She had a retentive memory, as well as a lively imagination. In the fashion of the day, she took home her finely scripted notes on Sunday sermons. One Sunday when John Alex was eight and sitting beside her sucking on a piece of horehound candy from her purse, she was brought to full attention by the text of the day from Isaiah: "Enlarge the place of thy tent, and let them stretch forth the curtains of thine habitations: spare not, lengthen thy cords, and strengthen thy stakes."

Isaiah had declaimed in these metaphors foreseeing a time under the Lord when Israel would expand its territory and power. The Reverend Mr. Filshey, rector of St. Alban's Anglican Church, chose the text to support his homily on the need to support mission work in Africa. Joanna savoured it as a colourful, and memorable way of keeping before herself the dream that indeed the day would come when her only child would go farther – take the family name farther – and enlarge the place of the Tyrone tent.

It was she, then, who first sowed the seed that grew in John Alex to become a mental and emotional fixation of his adult years. One hot July afternoon when he was eight and they were shelling green peas in the summer kitchen, she suddenly stopped, and looking at him with the full force of a mother's love, said "Your father made his mark and established the mill, but you will have an opportunity to do even better and pass on something better still to your children." It was his first encounter with the adult world of ambition and success, and bewildering at the time.

In the coming years John Alex would owe the stolidity in his character to William and the Tyrone side. From Joanna and the Strabane side, he inherited his underlying fire. He dated the beginning of his sense of destiny back to that hot July day of 1900 in the summer kitchen where he shelled peas with his mother.

Having planted the seed, Joanna never lost an opportunity to water it, pointing her son to the accomplishments of great men like King David and Abraham Lincoln. She loved maxims and proverbs and preferred them to the naked moralizing of 'you can... you should... you will.'

From John Alex' first school days, she directed his attention to the proverbs reproduced in his school reader, of which her favourite was that of wise King Solomon:

Go to the ant thou sluggard consider her ways and be wise;
Which having no guide, overseer, or ruler,
Provideth her meat in the summer,

14

and gathereth her food in the harvest.

She considered it as much her daily duty to build up his consciousness of what could lay ahead, as it was her duty to dispense his daily teaspoon of cod-liver oil.

Her memory was stocked with sayings that could be recovered as occasion required: *Lost time is never found again... Patience is the best remedy for every trouble... An empty bag cannot stand upright.*

When he left home her letters generally included a maxim or two. As a soldier in 1915 fighting in Flanders, his only belly laugh was triggered by one of these in which she extolled the virtues of personal hygiene and tailed-off with the words of the old saw that 'Cleanliness is next to Godliness.' At the time, he was standing ankle deep in mud that caked his khaki uniform and puttees.

The Tyrone grandparents, Alexander and Jane, had long been resting in Lilac Hill Cemetery, but the Strabane grandparents, Donald and Margaret, looked with pride and affection on young John.

Grandpa Strabane enjoyed taking the eight-year-old boy into his store and cluttered office with its gigantic roll-top desk. Before the clerks, Billy Dempster and Zenith Ball, he would compare young Tyrone to the boy's Uncle Charley. "Just like him. Regular tow head. Feel the muscle. He will pitch for Humber Bend, mark my words". To which, Billy would gravely nod his assent, "You couldn't .be righter, Mr. Strabane".

Grandma Strabane was much less interested in John Alexander's physical attributes and possibilities than in his moral and spiritual development. With Mrs. Minty, she shared a very lively sense of the glories of heaven and the horrors of hell. She made it her business to have her grandson included when the rector, the Reverend Mr. Filshey, made his quarterly call on them.

At such times, Strabane would not go into the store after lunch, but put on fresh clothes and compose himself for the trial of getting through the rector's sustained silences and penetrating glances, as he sipped his tea and helped himself to another tart. These visits were the only time the "little" parlour was opened and the velvet curtains beside the never-played harmonium were pulled aside to admit the light of day.

"This is a fine lad, Mrs. Strabane, can he recite the creed?"

"Yes rector, he can, and more. Repeat the Twenty-Third Psalm for the rector, John Alexander".

Anticipating this quarterly visit Grandma Strabane had added to the inducement of the tea and tarts the attraction of a reward of ten cents ("just a secret between the two of us") for a perfect performance before the man of God.

"Well done and perfectly spoken," said the rector, when John Alex had finished by slightly raising his voice to an affirmative pitch for the ending 'and I shall dwell in the house of the Lord forever'.

"With that kind of elocution you can go far in this world," the rector averred, "But tell me boy, what does this mean 'Thou preparest a table before me in the presence of mine enemies?' "

John Alex, beyond committing to memory all of the verses, wasn't prepared for this exigency and it wasn't until Grandpa Strabane, sitting to one side of Mr. Filshey, jerked his thumb in the direction of the large picture over the harmon-

16

ium in which King William of Orange was depicted crossing the Boyne on his white horse, that he could find his tongue and blurt out in a half voice, "God looks after us even when we is surrounded by Catholics".

"When we *are* surrounded by Catholics," corrected the rector, "and there are many other enemies that we must know about, but that can wait for another day." Then, with the self-assured air of one who had long ago mastered the art of bringing pastoral calls to a close, the rector extracted his gold watch from the slit in his vest and with a click of the filigreed case, cleared his throat and said, "Well, well, what do you know it's after four and I have a vestry meeting at five. Shall we kneel for a prayer?"

★   ★   ★

"What did the rector ask you today?" asked Joanna, as John Alex came onto the veranda where she was busy mending socks.

"He asked about our enemies."

"Our enemies, that's odd."

"Yes, why does God preparest a table before me in the presence of mine enemies."

"Ah, I see, and what did you say?

"I said God looks after us even when we is surrounded by Catholics."

"And what did the rector say to that?"

"He said, 'When we *are* surrounded by Catholics and we have other enemies too."

"Good grief son, I wonder if it's all as bad as that. Amy says that in Toronto some people have Catholics living on their very same street and there isn't any trouble. In her very last letter she says that when Dan was coming home, just the day before, a team of runaway horses came down Keele Street lickety-split and a Catholic woman ran in front of them to pull a young Protestant boy out of the way..."

Joanna voice trailed off as the two of them let the import of this news have its way. After a few moments their eyes were drawn to the road where Mr. Minty and other powdery figures were striding towards home. "The mill's shut down," said Joanna, "time for you to wash for supper."

★　　★　　★

John Alex started Humber Bend School at age six and for three years sat under Mr. Demeter Smith, a distant cousin of his mother. At the time, Mr. Smith was much distracted in his thoughts by Miss Mary Ann Semple, the banker's daughter, and because of this, the rigour required in his profession suffered. Nevertheless, he had a natural, flowing and elegant script. John Alex loved the hours spent on penmanship. Years later, when he went to work for Noah Oldfield in West Toronto Junction, his employer expressed approval of his ledger entries with the cryptic comment, "You got a good hand, son."

Through the remainder of his schooling at Humber Bend, he was under Mr. Joseph McCaul, a taciturn man – very exacting in his spelling and arithmetic drills – whose views and eccentricities left a lasting impression on John Alex.

In Senior Fourth, he was winning spelling contests in Humber Bend and beyond. At the provincial championship in Toronto, held at the Canadian Industrial Exhihition, he came second to another Senior Fourth pupil, Jessica Oldfleld, the daughter of his future employer. The decisive word, which might, had he spelt it correctly, given him a chance at the title was "euphony", which he misspelt "euphonie". Still, not only his parents, but many others from the village of Humber Bend took great satisfaction in the young Tyrone's scholarly distinction at the Ex.

There was, however, a danger in this excellence which came to his older half-brother Watt's attention when a group of boys, on their way to school across the bridge below the mill, taunted in voices calculated to carry "Too bad about John Alex he used to be a regular fella."

"Yeah, but now he's turning into teacher's pet."

"John Alex is lily livered, he can't beat his way out of a wet paper bag."

Watt was incensed. "Those young buggers," he muttered. At the time, Watt was twenty-six and living in his own house on Second Street with his wife Ella. Their first child was on the way and Watt had already assumed much of the management of both the mill and farm.

There wasn't anything passive in Watt's make-up. This challenge had to be met head on. But how? William was in his sixty-third year and while he was fond of John Alex he was largely oblivious to what was going on in the boy's life. As for Joanna, Watt didn't want her to be a part of his plans for he knew she held an unfavourable opinion of those families whose sons were seen smoking outside the black-smith's or using language that was unbecoming when it wasn't obscene (and certainly such that could never be used in polite company or in the presence of ladies). Nor did he want Mr. Minty, the mill foreman, to have any say in the matter.

As sure as God made green apples, Mr. Minty, like his wife, would spout something pious like "train up a child in the way he should go, and when he is old he will not depart from it" or "fear not them which kill the body but cannot kill the soul..."

★   ★   ★

From childhood, Watt had been in awe of Angus MacSpadden, the blacksmith. Everyone knew that Anvil (his nickname) was his own man. In his shop, he was the sole master regardless of whose horse was being shod or flange shaped. He shaved only on Sundays, a day he spent in rest, reading the Humber Bend Advertiser. Other than the occasional funeral, he saved his attendance at the Presbyterian Church for the annual Old Year's and Watch Night Service.

With a gelding's fetlock braced between his legs, Anvil was a picture of surgical deftness as he cleaned and pared the hoof and drove home the nails in the shoe. At such times, summer and winter, the sweat poured down onto his leather apron stained with the juice of an ever present tobacco quid, whose brown juice ran in tiny rivulets from the corner of his mouth and down over the graying stubble on his chin. It was said that Anvil could shoe twenty horses in the course of a working day, but normally he shod about four in the morning and four in the afternoon.

No one had ever thrown Anvil to the ground in a wrestling match, or pressed his wrist to the table in a test of arm strength. For all that, he was gentle and soothing with fractious animals and his way of saying "Easy girl" or "Stand boy" became the standard form of address to restive horses by his younger admirers. He was the only blacksmith in the county who could handle the flighty, blind team of drivers owned by E.G. Toplady, Esq., proprietor of the Victoria Hotel.

Knowing Anvil to be a busy man, and knowing that he would be at home on Sunday afternoon reading the Advertiser, Watt made his move. When he was admitted by Mrs. MacSpadden into the summer kitchen (the door to the front hall was never opened), he found Anvil sitting in his large chair at the kitchen table, the paper stretched before him.

"Good day Tyrone, and what brings you here on a Sabbath afternoon?"

"I have a family problem, Anvil."

"Yes, and what could that be?"

"Its about young John Alex."

"John Alex the spelling wonder?"

"Yes"

"And what's his problem, or your problem with him?"

After a pause, and looking out the window over Anvil's shoulder, Watt continued.

"Some of the young boys, and some that ain't so young, want to give John Alex a hard time. He was pushed down the river bank the other day coming home from school and a bunch of them pelted him with mud."

"Pushed him down... pelted... why the little..."

"Mind your tongue, Angus," cut in Mrs. MacSpadden.

"But did you hear Hattie what Tyrone said? Pushed him down the river bank... pelted him with mud!" Looking at Watt, "Do you know the reason for this?"

"Only that they can get away with it because he won't fight, and he's strong as an ox."

Anvil looked into the Advertiser as though he was expecting a revelation that would speak to his offended sense of justice. At first, nothing appeared beyond the usual advertisements for livestock and farm machinery, and then, just as Watt was beginning to think that Anvil didn't want to pursue the matter, his thick index finger came down on the socials column:

Come one come all to the Fourth Annual Highland Games, MacLaughlin's Flats, *Saturday, June 17, 4 o'clock Feats of Strength, Pipe Music, Refreshments for All Ages, Admission 25 cents, Children Come Free*

"Tell you what Tyrone, let me think about this. Come back next Sunday."

"Thanks Anvil, I'm sure you'll come up with something." And with a few words of parting, Watt was on his way. As he passed out the door, Hattie MacSpadden, sitting with her tattered Psalter, muttered, "And since when did a Tyrone want advice from anyone?"

★　★　★

Angus MacSpadden was not one to equivocate, and when Watt came into his kitchen seven days later, he had a plan formulated.

"There's a way John Alex can pull himself up in the esteem of the boys."

"Anything you say," said Watt. "Tell me what you have in mind."

"Alright, I'll put it before you Tyrone. It come to me when I read the notice of the highland games at MacLaughlin's. Come the Glorious Twelfth of July, we is going to have our own highland games, and John Alex is the one who will be glorious."

"But Anvil," said Watt, "You're not even a Orangeman."

"That's so, but I always observe the holiday and this year I'm telling you there will be the Junior Highland Games sponsored by me, Angus MacSpadden, in the pasture across the creek behind my shop. Any boy, age twelve to sixteen, can enter and compete in the shot put and the caber contest."

A few days later a colourful poster appeared on the door of the blacksmith shop, another on the main door of the mill, and another in Strabane's store window facing Main Street:

Celebrate the Glorious 12th at

MAC SPADDEN'S JUNIOR HIGHLAND GAMES

Ages 12 to 16 can compete.

Prizes for caber, shot put, long jump, arm wrestling.

Starts at 2 o'clock sharp on the flats behind MacSpadden's blacksmith shop.

Rumour started to spread that Todd Wilson could easily dominate the games, who from an early age, could perform near marvels of strength and daring. At fourteen, he dropped out of school and took a job in his father's creamery where local farmers remarked on his capacity for hard work 'as good or better than any man'.

During June, the school had entered a drowsy stage after Arbour Day and as soon as it was let out, John Alex and Watt headed to the farm where at six o'clock, Anvil joined them to coach in the finer points of the caber fling, the shot put, and arm wrestling. The poster had not mentioned that, for the Junior Highland Games, the fearsome caber would not be used, but instead the ingenious blacksmith struck upon using a much reduced version in the form of a cedar fence post.

"John Alex," said Watt to his half-brother, "you like peace and you can't see the sense in fighting, but I'll tell you, some of the young buggers around Humber Bend will never respect you and leave you alone until you not only prove that you are smarter in the books, but also better in manly things."

The Twelfth of July, dawned bright, clear and hot. Following their usual breakfast of porridge, sausages, fried eggs and pie, the Tyrones readied themselves for the annual Orange parade on Main Street.

The fife band and the marchers of all ages in their whites with orange sashes formed up outside the Orange Hall on Maple Street, then following King Billy on his white horse turned down Main Street to the sound of the fife and drum. Then, taking Queen Street, then Elm Street, ended up again on Maple Street in front of the village bandstand.

This year, it was the turn of the Methodist minister to speak to those assembled, and after a hearty rendition of God Save the King, the Reverend John Wesley Borden, frequently mopping his brow with a linen handkerchief, meticulously laundered for the occasion, spoke for about forty minutes on the subject of 'A Protestant Bible, a Protestant Monarchy, and a Protestant People', while the thirstier element drifted away from the heat and the piety for the relief to be found within the cool taproom of the Victoria Hotel, or behind the Council drive-shed beside the river.

None of the Tyrones or Strabanes marched with the parade that year, although they all had some identification of orange in hair ribbons, hat bands and the like. Joanna herself wore an orange lily at the crest of her curved bodice. But, with the heat, and the long standing for the parade, and the Reverend Mr. Borden's address, she was relieved when Watt suggested that they all head home for dinner. John Alex would have to rest and do some warm-up exercises before going to MacSpadden's games.

Anvil had cordoned an area for the games, not so much for any other purpose than to hold back the more ribald and tipsy of those males who, unlike the Tyrones, had not gone home for dinner. It was hardly necessary, since even drunk men held Anvil in awe.

Down under the willows by the river, the persons who Joanna described as 'definitely not our kind' were drunkenly chorusing "Teeter-totter, holy water, hang the Pope and marry his daughter".

Shortly after two, Todd Wilson arrived with his younger brothers and friends. Shorty Fullerton, Donald Cronyn and Roly Peel, the tormentors of John Alex, registered at the box beside the cordon, as did the tormented one himself. Shorty elbowed Donald and winked at Roly.

Todd Wilson had only one competitor in his category, there were five in the fifteen year category, seven in the fourteen year category, and eleven in the thirteen year category. All were, or had been, pupils in the Humber Bend Public School.

It was decided that the competition would commence with the youngest and advance to the eldest. The twelve-year-olds couldn't do anything with the caber, but they managed to get a shot-put of a few yards, do the broad-jump and arm wrestle. Stuart McGroom took most of the points for this group.

Then it was the turn of the thirteen year olds. They were called out in alphabetical order. Shorty Fullerton was exceptional, steady in his control of the caber, easily passing the others with his shot-put and overcoming all of the others except John Alex in the arm wrestling. That sent a murmur around the ring of those behind the cordon. Then it was John Alex' turn. Watt called, "Take your time". Shorty and his chums looked on with faint humour.

Anvil instructed John Alex to take the caber. He easily balanced it before him in his two hands and his running fling went without strain a full yard beyond Shorty's. His shot-put fell barely ahead of Shorty's, but he came a foot ahead in the long jump.

For John Alex, Watt, and Anvil it *was* a Glorious Twelfth. Later, on total points, Todd Wilson was declared overall winner. As John Alex took his prize of a Sheffield pen-knife donated by Strabane's Hardware, he could feel in the surrounding silence of his peers their jealous respect. He was never taunted again in Humber Bend.

★   ★   ★

That year, William turned over the complete operation of the mill to Watt and contented himself, thereafter, with supervision of the farm where he bred Clydesdales. John Alex helped in the haying and harvest, but never much fancied the life of a farmer.

The following year, he completed all the education offered by the Humber Bend School. He stood at the head of the entrance class, as much the result of Joanna's prodding, as of his own initiative.

★   ★   ★

One afternoon in February, Watt directed John Alex to hitch Dolly and Prince to the bob-sleigh and collect a shipment of grain sacks off the 3:10 from Toronto. As he came abreast of the waiting room door, with his freight in the sleigh's box, the station master hailed him. "Gentleman warming himself by the stove wants a lift to the Victoria."

"Sure" said John Alex.

In a moment, he was inviting a tall, spare man with a black beard, a black homburg, a black muffler and a black coat to sit beside him. He was a total stranger and not inclined to conversation. Dolly and Prince trotted them into the village and up to the hotel without a word being exchanged between man and boy.

As the stranger stepped down, John Alex handed him his Gladstone bag and the stranger said, "Thank you boy, thank you," with a heavy accent.

Over supper, John Alex told Joanna of his experience. "Sounds to me like some kind of preacher. All in black and a black beard you say. Well son, there are no secrets in Humber Bend so we will learn before long who this stranger is."

Right after supper the next day, as William lit his pipe, Joanna said to John Alex, "That stranger you dropped at the hotel is a tailor from Toronto and he has come with samples of suiting. He intends to get orders here according to Mrs. Toplady. She says he is a Jew, the first to come to Humber Bend."

That Saturday the Advertiser had the following notice:
Mr. Jacob Fine, Tailor, of 384 Spadina Avenue, Toronto, is pleased to notify the gentlemen of Humber Bend and District that he will have samples of his superior woolens in various weights and will be taking orders for top coats and suits at the Victoria Hotel, Monday to Wednesday of this coming week (Feb. 15, 16, 17). Delivery is guaran-

teed within 60 days.

Joanna seldom looked at the Advertiser, so having given the matter a little forethought, it was William who suggested that John Alex be measured for a suit to start high school in Brampton.

Entering the end room on the second floor of the Victoria, John Alex found Jacob Fine in vest and shirt sleeves sitting behind a small table on which rested his order book, tape measure, and samples.

"Is you my driver? For you, is discount. How tall is you?"

"I'm six foot," said the youth.

"My Nathan should be so tall," said the tailor.

"Nathan, is he in high school?"

"Yes. He is also in Hebrew school. You know what is that?"

"I'm sorry, sir, I don't"

"Is where you learn Torah and Talmud, what God say, like you goyim call Bible."

"Oh... like religion."

"Yes... like religion... more boy, more, like life."

★   ★   ★

In the fall of that year, John Alex was boarded with his cousins Cecil and Edna Strabane on Elm Street in Brampton, where he remained, except for the summer recess, until he finished high school at the age of eighteen.

-1910-

In August of 1910, John Alex moved into the home of his sister Amy and her husband Dan in West Toronto Junction. Back in 1903, Amy had left the employ of Hattie Longford in Humber Bend to marry Dan MacLaren, the son of a Humber Bend farmer.

Dan worked for the Canadian Pacific Railway as an oiler in the roundhouse. By 1910, he had advanced to the status and dignity of a locomotive engineer, and was well on his way to paying off the mortgage on their modest home on Pacific Avenue.

To the MacLarens, John Alex was something of a model youth – quiet, polite, ambitious, and a non-drinker. He gave the appearance of having no particular interest in girls, not even pretty girls like Marjorie Stanton, whose father fired on the CPR. Amy invited Marjorie for Sunday dinner from time to time in John Alex' first year with them, but he was not stirred enough to pursue things beyond the table.

He was anxious to get a job and took every opportunity to follow leads pointing to suitable employment for someone with a high school diploma. In the fourth form, he had passed over the option of continuing his study of Latin, in favour of business practice. It was to be as a result of a chance conversation between Dan and Shorty Cooper, a foundry machinist, that a job prospect came into view.

*　　*　　*

From the time of expanding railway construction in the Toronto area and on past the War of 1914-1918, West Toronto Junction and its municipal successor West Toronto, continued to spread out with new streets, churches, schools and stores. Part of this was attractive, in a middle class way, with big brick houses standing behind well shaded lawns. On the northern perimeter of the Junction, humbler houses lined the streets nearer the railway tracks.

Not far from where the tracks crossed Keele Street, north of the shunting area, the sheds and pens of Siding Street handled freight off a short spur. Here cattle, grain and lumber from the hinterland were unloaded and fencing, machinery, hardware and much else were loaded for destinations across the country. Destined like so many other similar thoroughfares to remain unknown, save for the handful of men and women who worked there, Siding Street lay at the hub of great exchanges of wealth.

A converted day coach had been drawn up parallel to the street. The sign beneath the window read *Railway Restaurant Jos. Grogan, Esq., Prop.* The Grogan family had emigrated from Tipperary. As a young man, Joe Grogan went West on Canadian Pacific track gangs. In Winnipeg, he met and married Olga Pylipiw.

The Grogans were thrifty and ambitious and, by 1904 with savings from a small cafe they operated in Portage La Prairie, were able to move east and establish themselves on

30

Siding Street in West Toronto Junction, where the constant shunting of freight cars rattled the cups and saucers of their simple eatery, and the sound of engine yard whistles drowned out conversation.

Grogan's was popular with railroaders, drovers, teamsters and others whose work brought them onto Siding Street or beside it. It was here that Dan MacLaren made his way at various hours of the day or night for a coffee and fried egg sandwich.

Shorty Cooper worked for the Royal Spring and Axle Company, along the street from the diner, and he came into Grogan's on those days when Mrs. Cooper refused to speak to him or pack his lunch. He and Dan would frequently arrive in the diner at noon and fall into conversation about lacrosse or baseball. On one such occasion, Dan mentioned that his young brother-in-law who was boarding with him had excelled at lacrosse in Brampton, but so far hadn't got onto a team in Toronto. In fact, "right now he needs a job more'n he needs lacrosse."

"Your brother-in-law," asked Shorty, "what's he trained for?"

"Tells me he took bookkeeping in Fourth Form."

"That so... do you know that old man Oldfield is looking for a bookkeeper right now, as we speak. Red Irish has to quit, been with the old man for years, his cough's bad."

The next day, John Alex was admitted to Noah Oldfield's office at Royal Spring and Axle. Oldfield was at his roll-top desk crammed with papers. As he spoke, his words were shouted to overcome the din of the works just beyond his office wall.

"What can I do for you?" he asked, while simultaneously aiming a squirt of tobacco spittle at his cuspidor.

"I understand you will need a bookkeeper," shouted John Alex. "I have taken a Fourth Form honour in that subject."

"Who told you I need a bookkeeper? Yes I do, matter of fact, this your first run at getting a job?"

"Yes sir, this is my first application in the city," said John Alex, crushing the brim of a new black fedora. "I'm eighteen, just graduated in June and moved to the Junction from Humber Bend in July." After musing for what to John Alex seemed an eternity, and swivelling back and forth before his desk, occasionally ousting further brown jets towards the cuspidor, Oldfield finally said, "You seem a sturdy and smart sort. Did whoever told you I needed a bookkeeper, tell you that our bookkeeper is also the timekeeper and the pay-master?"

"No sir, but I'm sure I can learn. Saw how it was done at our mill in Humber Bend."

Oldfield stopped swivelling and drawled, "That so... that so," and after a further pause, all the time eyeing John Alex thoughtfully, he said "Tell you what... come in for a month on probation and learn from Mr. Irish whose leaving... You don't mind he has a bad cough? If, in a month, we think you can handle the job – it's yours when Mr. Irish retires. That suit you?"

"Yes sir," said John Alex, relaxing his grip on the fedora's brim.

"We open our doors at seven and close at six, except on Saturdays when we leave at four. Come through and meet Mr. Irish." Oldfield was already leading the way to the outer office.

John Alex enjoyed the walk each morning from the MacLarens' on Pacific Avenue to the works on Siding Street. He was careful to always arrive, as the front door was being unlocked by Oldfield at fifteen before seven, when a number of the blue collar workers also arrived by the factory door and punched their time cards. The works' whistle blew at seven and in a matter of a few minutes, the clang of forged steel, the screeching of drills, the whine of grinders and the entire cacophony of the works, penetrated into the office. It filled the air as far as the Grogans' diner and beyond, competing with the clanking and chuffing of railway engines in the nearby yards. The noise silenced with the whistle announcing noon, leaving only the remoter railway sounds to fill the void.

Along with the freight sheds and pens, a number of small enterprises suckled at the side of the railway spur – a nourishing location for sack and twine manufacturing, slaughter houses, and tanneries. Among the low slung buildings that housed these activities, the red brick Royal Spring and Axle foundry works stood out with its large windows, false front and vertical skylights. Designed and built by Noah Oldfield, it was much the most prominent structure on the street. Oldfield took pride in it and every fortnight had the works' sign-board over the front office scrubbed clean of its grime by the day shift fireman, Henry.

In a way, the Tyrone mill had prepared John Alex for the foundry interior with its driveline, belts and pulleys – here, powered by a coal-fired steam generator, instead of a mill race. He found, too, that the buggy-spring making area was simply MacSpadden's blacksmith shop writ large with two forges and anvils, instead of one of each. The press punch and riveter were new to him. The axle room also had novelty because he had never seen a tempering furnace or a nibbler for sizing axles. But overall, if he closed his eyes he could think easily of MacSpadden's because of the banging, the heat, the dust, the hissing of hot metal being cooled in vats, and the smell.

That summer of his probation John Alex listened... often forced himself to listen... to Mr. Irish's explanations of the many entries in the Royal Spring and Axle Company's ledgers. The bookkeeper was in pitiable shape, bringing up blood into his handkerchief. In little more than a month, after he left the office in early September, he was dead.

On the Civic Holiday, August 4, Oldfield released his workers for the day, as he himself intended to take the holiday excursion by train to Niagara Falls with his wife Stella, daughter Jessica, and son Jimmy. John Alex seized the opportunity for a visit to Humber Bend and took his Sunday clothes to work with him on Saturday in Dan's Gladstone bag. After work, he raced to the station just in time to catch the 4:20 for Humber Bend.

When he went in by the summer kitchen, he was greeted by Joanna with open arms. William looked on bemused through wreaths of pipe smoke and asked, "How is it son... how's the city?"

John Alex disengaged from his mother's embrace and said, "Dan and Amy are fine. My employer is Mr. Noah Old-field and he has a works for making buggy-axles and springs on Siding Street near the station. Gave us all the Civic Holiday. I'm to be the company bookkeeper when Mr. Irish retires. He has an awful cough, even brings up blood."

"An awful cough, did you say?" spurted Joanna, "and are

34

you sitting close to him? I don't want you to get consumption, God in heaven forbid."

"No, no, Momma. Don't worry, I'm careful to keep clean and wash. Besides Mr. Irish is leaving next month. He has been very kind and patient... How are Watt and the family?"

"Fine, fine. Watt misses you. Ella is expecting. Young Kenny is a terror."

"Mother," said William "let's have some supper for this boy."

*   *   *

On Monday, during the relative quiet of noon, John Alex was reading the lacrosse news in the Mail and Empire, his lunch pail open before him, when a young woman stepped confidently through the office door and immediately said, "And how are you today Mr. Tyrone?"

"I'm, uh, fine," said John Alex.

"You don't know who I am, but Poppa has told me about you."

"He has?"

"Yes, I know all about you."

"You do?"

"I sometimes take the deposit to the bank for Miss Henty."

"You do..."

"I just said I did. You don't happen to know where I can find the deposit bag?"

"It's in the safe, of course."

"*It's in the safe, of course.* But can't you get it?"

"Sorry, I don't know the combination and both your

35

father and Miss Henty are not here just now."

She stood by the window and bent slightly to glance towards Grogan's. He sat motionless, a fine sweat coming out on his forehead. His celluloid collar felt like a ring of steel, his sandwich rested forgotten on the Mail and Empire.

She turned, and fingering the hair that fell over her shoulder, said "I thought you would remember me."

"Remember you. Sorry Miss Oldfield."

"Jessica. I prefer Jessica."

"Jessica..."

"The spelling bee for senior fourths at the Exhibition – Jessica Oldfield, first prize; John Alexander Tyrone, second prize...You do remember."

"Ahhh! But you look different."

"Six years different Mr. Tyrone."

"John Alexander...Johnny to my friends."

At that point, both of them glimpsed Noah Oldfield as he came into view crossing the dusty ruts of Siding Street. It was the beginning of September, 1910.

★   ★   ★

As Noah Oldfield stepped off the street into the outer office of Royal Spring and Axle, he gave John Alex a look without breaking stride and entered his own office. In short order, he dispatched Jessica with the bank deposit.

Some of the business people in the Junction found Noah a trifle rough. He had not been privileged to go beyond the Third book. What he knew, he learned in the proverbial school of hard knocks, mostly in other small foundries similar to his own. What he lacked in 'book learning', he compensated by rigorous attention to detail, keen observation, and frugality.

He was also a shrewd investor and land speculator. When the bloom faded on the Junction's development in the mid-1890s he purchased some lots from the municipality for next to nothing at auction. These he judiciously held until home-building recommenced and sold off at up to double his purchase cost. It was from this speculation, as well as profit he allowed himself out of Royal Spring and Axle, that he was able to build a substantial five-bedroom home on Annette Street, a few blocks west of the CPR station.

Within the Annette Street residence, Stella Oldfield ruled. She came from a prosperous farming family in Oxford County, and had completed two years of high school in Woodstock. While she could afford a domestic, she insisted on doing all the work in the house herself, rising with her husband every morning at 5:30 and following a cleaning, cooking and shopping routine from Monday to Saturday that only lapsed for family reunions, church socials, funerals and weddings. Evenings she devoted to her mending and reading, enjoying her leather bound copies of Scott, Poe, Longfellow, and Stevenson, as well as her cheaper cloth bound copies of Susannah Moody's *Roughing it in the Bush* and Ralph Connor's *Glengarry School Days*.

Stella gave birth to two children and had one miscarriage. Both of her live babies were delivered by Dr. A.C. Mavety in the front bedroom of their first Junction residence on Keele Street; Jessica in 1893 and Jimmy in 1900. It was a crushing blow, when some weeks after Jimmy's birth, Mavety told the parents that their son would not develop normally.

The Oldfields had yearned for the gift of a son through the years. Before Mavety passed judgment on Jimmy's future, they already suspected the worst. After this, and for many days, they spoke to each other in lowered voices. A stillness prevailed in the house which Jessica at the age of seven could sense.

One night, she awoke to the sounds of sobs coming from her parents' bedroom. In the morning, Stella came down to prepare breakfast red eyed and pale. Jessica followed her brisk movements, while listlessly spooning up porridge, prompting Stella to blurt, "Get a move on child, or you're going to be late for school."

Each afternoon, Jimmy was taken upstairs for his rest. One Saturday when it was time for him to be fed, Jessica heard him crying and went up to his nursery to find Stella staring absently out the window. "It's alright," Stella said gently, without turning. Then facing her daughter, added tearfully, "A little crying is good for Jimmy's lungs... he won't ever be like other children, you know."

In the evenings, Noah came in and immediately took Jimmy into his arms. On Siding Street, he was known as one who didn't suffer fools gladly. Sluggardly suppliers were given the full brunt of his wrath by phone or letter. But Jimmy lived to the age of thirty-two and never heard an impatient word from his father.

★   ★   ★

The Fentons, Walter and Joan, were Oldfields' neighbours, two doors to the west. Robina was a classmate and confidente of Jessica's. Her younger twin brothers, Stanley and Frank, were robust and outgoing.

When the Fenton boys were about ten or eleven their father made them a rickshaw using the shafts and front wheels of a light buggy. Stanley pulled Frank and Frank pulled Stanley. They gave Robina and Jessica a ride after school.

"Mrs. Oldfieid, can Jimmy take a ride?"

"Jimmy? Is it safe?"

"Dad made it, it's strong!"

"Yes, I know your dad is a good mechanic... but will Jimmy fall off?"

"Naw, Frank and me is strong. Look at this muscle on my arm. Frank will pull and I'll hold Jimmy tight."

"Well, just a little ride... down to the church and back."

"Come on, Jimmy. You're going for a ride. Hold my hand. That's it. Hold on tight. Git up, Frank. Git up."

This entertainment for Jimmy and the twins continued frequently through the summer days. Stella kept her eye on the trip through the lace curtain in the front bay window. She made a quick flight into the street, in the latter part of August when three bigger boys, on their way to a ball game, tried to wrest the shafts out of Frank's hands and practically jerked Stanley and Jimmy from the seat onto the road. At the sight of Stella beating down on them, the interlopers retreated, but not without a few taunts thrown over their shoulders.

The sport palled by month's end and after Labour Day the rickshaw disappeared, never to re-appear.

★   ★   ★

"Mother," said Noah, one morning the· following spring, "The Grand Lodge is having a service in St. James' Cathedral on Victoria Day. I will be·seated, as usual, with the brethren, but I want all of us to be there and to be seen. I want you and Jessica to get something new for this. I'm

39

getting a new cutaway at Chisholm's and it's time Jimmy got his next suit. I thought he'd bust out of his jacket at Easter."

Stella was pleased, but not so that it would show, "I tried to tell you that some time ago, but you weren't listening, were you?"

"Well, mother..."

"Don't 'well mother' me. For some time we have over-done simplicity around here. Will there be anyone I know?"

"I dare say. I dare say. Some of the nabobs from Oxford County are coming."

At this point, Jessica, age fifteen at the time, came into the dining room pinafored neatly for school. As she finished her second piece of johnnycake drowned in maple syrup, Stella called from the kitchen, "Jessica, something important has come up... I'm going to cancel your lesson on Saturday with Miss Ogilvie. We're going downtown."

"Downtown, Momma?"

"Downtown... well, not quite downtown... In fact, to Darling's."

"Darling's?"

"Yes, the dress and millinery store on College Street"

On Saturday morning, Noah brought the Model-T up to the curb at nine. The Fenton boys had been delighted to earn a shinplaster cleaning it. Jimmy was first in and bizooing the horn to Stella's consternation, as she straightened her hat before the hall mirror.

On the way to Darling's, Jimmy was in perpetual motion, pulling the back seat blind, raising and lowering the foot rail... Jessica's remonstrances being of little effect.

Darling's (The Store for Women) carried an exhaustive stock of yard goods in its floor to ceiling shelves. Five seamstresses and two milliners worked in a section partitioned off at the back. Troy Darling managed the business from his office adjoining the sewing area.

Adele Darling and assistant, Ena Belvedere, attended to customers who required dress-fittings. Three other women were placed behind the long oak counter, with its inset brass rule, serving the constant traffic of women who came in off College Street through the brass revolving door. The fitting room was situated beside the owner's office. It was small, elegant, with a triptych of gilt-framed mirrors, a rich carpet, and plush chairs.

Conscious of what was expected of her, Stella sat erectly, fingering a copy of Harper's Bazaar, while Jessica stood nervously before her.

Mrs. Darling held the end of a bolt across Jessica's shoulders of a floral pattern with cream background. She gave the effect an appreciative appraisal through her lorgnette, and after a pause said, "It's the finest toile de Jouy we have, madam. Perfect for spring. See how it complements the young lady's brown eyes...

"Yes, that will do," clipped Stella.

"May I suggest too, madam, that we follow the pattern that madam will see in the illustration on page nineteen... very, very au courant... And, one final suggestion: Let us cut the bodice a little loose to allow for further natural development this year without tightness."

When Stella and Jessica rejoined Noah and·Jimmy in the car, Noah asked, "What will that cost?"

"Enough," replied Stella dryly.

"Poppa, it's beautiful," said Jessica radiantly. "And my hat will have a little bird on it."

There was a sudden hullabaloo down the street. The passing window shoppers turned just in time to see the lead horses fling out of the fire hall a block away. The team of six came towards the Oldfields at full gallop and as the fire-pumper swerved by them, an unbattened nozzle caught under the Model-T, and before the violent forward thrust of the horses and pumper could dislodge, the car was on the curb and the gas tank had sprung a leak.

The shoppers, affronted by the impact of gasoline fumes, moved quickly away. But, a corpulent fellow, cigar clenched in teeth, stood his ground towards the curb.

"Back! back!" shouted Noah. "Do you want to blow us all to kingdom come?"

As the man stepped back into the crowd, now gathering at some distance, Stella and Jessica with handkerchiefs over their noses, and Jimmy in tow, moved towards Darling's revolving door. They were badly shaken and Jimmy kept repeating "Bad horses. Bad men. Bad horses. Bad men. Bad, bad, bad." Noah stared at the car akimbo over the sidewalk. "Blast" he muttered.

Two constables arrived, and stood with stolid deference, as Noah told them what had happened. "Will you be pressing charges?" one of them asked.

"Pardon me, sir," said a youth who had suddenly appeared beside Noah.

"Yes, what?"

"I know a man near here who will come and get this fixed for you."

"What kind of a man?"

"My uncle. He has a smith shop. Torch. Tools. Everything."

"Go and get him, and be quick."

A fine April rain started to fall. Troy Darling came out to the street nudged by his partner wife. "Please come in," he said. "The ladies are getting tea. Why do these things have to happen? But don't worry, that boy is good stuff and so are his family. They will do right by you."

"What is their name?" asked Noah.

"Fine is their name. The old man has a tailor shop on Spadina. Does good work. We send him a little trade now and then."

It was forty-five minutes later that a light wagon appeared with the youth and a bearded man in leather apron.

"This is not hard," said the man, pulling out the front seat to get to the tank. "Just take it to the shop for welding."

Jessica came out to the street with Noah. She was intrigued, particularly by the youth with his thick black eyebrows, compact figure, and serious expression. At first, he was too focussed on his uncle's work with disconnecting the tank to notice her gaze, but when he finally turned his glance to the sidewalk, he was taken aback by her riveting stare. As their eyes met, he smiled in friendly acknowledgement. She smiled back, and then with a tingle of excitement running through her, and a blush mounting in her face, she turned and hurried into the store.

1914 – 1918

The ring of farms and villages to the east of the old city was already choked with carnage when the Germans opened the Second Battle of Ypres on April 14, 1915. By mid-May, Ypres was destroyed and the saddened world heard of the first use of poison gas in warfare. On April 22, Algerian tirailleurs scrambled into the view of the Canadians gasping "gaz... gaz". The attack of the 22nd was followed by another on the 24th, and badly damaged the Canadians themselves, who nevertheless managed to hold on.

John Alex and the Fenton boys, as part of the Toronto Regiment, were with the 3rd Brigade, ordered to hold Mouse Trap Farm – also known as Shelltrap and Death Farm. Close to Ypres, it was a link in the Allies' line, which ran along Paschendale Ridge, through Hill 60 and Sanctuary Wood to Paschendale Village.

The Second Battle of Ypres claimed 10,000 Canadian lives by the end of June. Officers and men were constantly raised in rank in the field to keep command structure. After only two weeks at Mouse Trap, John Alex was raised from lieutenant to captain. On one of the short rushes towards the enemy, from the trenches between Mouse Trap Farm and the village of St. Julian, John Alex fell into the mud, his left leg limp under blood-soaked putties. The next day, during a similar foray, Frank and Stanley Fenton were killed by enemy fire, mere yards apart.

Through murderous fire, the stretcher-bearers carried John Alex back to Brigade Headquarters at Mouse Trap. The straw in the courtyard was covered with the wounded. Captain Hayward, the Toronto Regiment's MO, worked around the clock, blood to his elbows, in the makeshift operating room set up in the old farmhouse. There was nothing he could do for John Alex but drug down the emerging pain, cut away breeches and putties, and staunch the flow of blood with gauze and bandages. The next day, he was moved into an old chateau overlooking the Somme River – now converted to a military hospital by the French.

Coming out of his morphine haze, John Alex was first aware of shafts of sunlight descending on the rows of bandaged and groaning men. Nursing sisters were whisking about between the cots and down the aisles. A major of the Royal Medical Corps and a nursing sister came through together. She read her case notes with an air of authority beside each of the wounded as they progressed, Anglicizing the names of the Algerians, who had been caught in the gas and shrapnel at St. Julian. They were beyond caring.

"This is Captain Tyrone, C Company, Canadian 3rd Brigade, shattered right knee, wounds cleaned and dressed, bone splinters removed by Captain Pearce, splints and bandages as required."

"Thank you, Sister," said the major. "How are you, Captain? Close one, eh? It's back to Blighty for you, and you can be damn thankful."

John Alex had to lie motionless. The slightest movement brought shocks of pain from the smashed knee. He had recently started to smoke as an antidote for the misery of trench warfare. Holding his cigarette clear of the cot, he followed its ascending wisp of smoke with his eyes, but his mind was elsewhere. He had no desire to talk. Just as well, since his neighbours were all French-speaking, and his French hardly stretched beyond "Parlez-vous anglais?"

The weeks spent in the Ypres Salient were weeks in the mouth of Hell: the cold, the mud, the lice, the stench, the damp, the rats – and above all, the noise. Even worse was the having to live in constant dread that your number would soon be up and your name added to those killed or missing in action. As put by one private, "You go into the line like a filly on green grass. You come out like a carcass for the glue factory."

As John Alex' head cleared, his relief at being alive was tinged with guilt. God, how sweet life is. But, why me? Why not the Fenton boys, who only a year ago were playing lacrosse in West Toronto? Why not all the others of the Toronto Regiment – strong men, healthy men, now felled forever by the bombardments and machine gun fire of April and May. What, he wondered, had become of the new officers commissioned at Mouse Trap. Where were they?

Of the war itself, while it was hell, it never entered John Alex' mind to question its legitimacy. The Hun had walked over little Belgium and what would he do next if he wasn't stopped. He had to be stopped! "Damn the conshies and socialists and pacifists," he reasoned. "All a pack of cowards and laggards. The girls did the right thing to hand them white feathers. Germany was a sneak and a bully and it needed, above all, a lesson in straight dealing by British steel."

His regiment was now engaged in the Battle of Mount Sorel, but he was effectively out of action for the duration. He had his 'Blighty' and in the first week of May was shipped via Calais and Shornecliffe to a hospital in Kent. Like the chateau hospital overlooking the Somme, Queen's Hill, midway between Maidstone and Canterbury, had a manorial past. It had been turned over to the Ministry of Defence as a convalescent hospital during the First Battle of Ypres. During his stay at Queen's Hill, the Australians made their sacrificial landing in Gallipoli; the Lusitania was torpedoed; disclosure of a munitions supply scandal enraged Westminster; and London experienced its first zeppelin air bombardment.

In the officers' ward at Queen's Hill, John Alex started to regain his zest for life and to consciously bury the ugliness of the Front. For its part, the hospital consciously tried to spread cheerfulness and dispel gloom. A parade of ventriloquists, church choirs and slapstick entertainers performed for the wounded in the grand front hall.

He was dozing when he was brought to by a gentle tap on the shoulder.

"Captain Tyrone?" It was a young lieutenant speaking.

"Yes."

"Greetings from General Turner. You and two other officers of the 3rd Brigade are to be decorated. Recommendation passed up by Major Kirkpatrick.

"Good God, that so?"

"Yes sir, today at 14:00 hours. Here, put away those Woodbines. Try one of my Sweet Caps. Nothing like a Canadian cigarette when you have been over here for a bit."

At precisely 14:00 hours, the General arrived on the

ward – now silent as a cat's breath – led by the young lieutenant and the Sister in charge. Staff stood along the wall and those patients who could, sat up on the edge of their beds, or craned their necks where they were lying in order to watch.

The General's deep voice was conversational: "Having yourself a Blighty, Captain?"

"Yes sir, I guess so."

"Not like some though, the real thing."

"Yes sir."

"Pain?"

"Lots of pain, sir."

"Family. Write to them?"

"Yes sir."

Without further ado, the General, a man of few words, read from a folded vellum sheet passed to him by the lieutenant:

> *Captain John Alexander Tyrone is awarded the Military Cross for bravery under fire and outstanding leadership during the action of 23 April, 1915, near St. Julien, Flanders, where he repeatedly exposed himself to enemy fire in the effort to close the gap between the 2nd Battalion of the 3rd Brigade, 1st Canadian Division, and the village of St. Julien.*

★   ★   ★

John Alex had crossed a bridge – amazingly and incredulously. One of the very lucky ones – he knew that. Flanders and the war itself lay behind him. Staring at the vaulted roof of the ward, he struggled to put it all out of his mind, going back to Humber Bend and back to West

49

Toronto, only to have the horror break upon him.

At times, he had a sensation of peace as though floating in the punt on the mill pond at home − chiefly after his nightly sedative. Then all hell broke loose. The pond was sucked into a vortex with the punt, and the terrified soldier − the sky blackened and canons roared.

A month on, he was still immobilized in a thigh-to-ankle cast, but able to sit up in bed with a pillow at his back. He was filled with admiration and appreciation for the nursing sisters − their swift ease in bathing him, changing his sheets and puffing up his pillow. They loved to tease the 'Canadian gentleman', and he was flattered.

He stared out the window of the hospital on the languishing rose beds and neglected lawn − his mind turning to Jessica.

At first their relationship had been smooth, then sputtered, and then was smooth again. He smiled thinking of it. Joanna Tyrone, speaking to a friend about her son, said that "Still waters run deep." Indeed, it had taken him some time to clear the hurdle of his reserve, and express to Jessica his feelings for her. Actually, it was Jessica who made the first move after their initial encounter in the office of Royal Spring and Axle.

"Momma, have you met Poppa's new bookkeeper?"

"No. Your father says he is a bright young fellow. Home's in Humber Bend."

"Do you think he is lonely, Momma? I mean with his home in Humber Bend."

"Possibly," she said, as a quizzical and mildly amused look came across her face, "possibly."

"Wouldn't it be nice to have him for dinner some

Sunday, or over for supper some evening?"

"I understand he goes to lacrosse games," and then Stella added, "You arrange something."

From suppers and dinners, the relationship moved on to boating on Grenadier Pond in the summer, and skating on the pond in winter. He was captivated by her. Totally infatuated. Moreover, to him her infectious laughter and natural elegance was like that of his mother Joanna, whose charm was still able to draw envious female glances as she glided down Main Street in Humber Bend to do her shopping.

After tea, they always had tea with a biscuit in mid-afternoon at Queen's Hill – his mind went back to Jessica. She entered Victoria University in the autumn of 1910. It was shortly after that he began feeling that their romance lost traction. Suddenly, she was earnest and passionate about things that were foreign to him – socialism, pacifism, temperance, suffragism. By contrast, his world was bounded by work, lacrosse, militia training, and the Blue Lodge of Freemasonry.

It was something of a shock to him that Jessica was going off on a tangent from what he thought was normal. Had he been more astute, he would have had some fore-warning from his discussions with Stella Oldfield, who was of a very independent mind. This independent mind carried her into the leadership of both the Women's Christian Temperance Union, and the Imperial Order of the Daughters of the Empire in West Toronto. He should also have had an indication of the nascent Oldfield feminism when .it became obvious that it was Stella and Jessica combined who held out for university over Noah's objection that it was better for girls to take clerical and secretarial courses.

"Why shouldn't she?" demanded Stella, "She finished

with honours and she has as much intelligence or more than most young men, including your protégé Johnny Tyrone." And that was that.

On a Friday evening in late February, John Alex met Jessica at the end of the streetcar line to walk her home. She was in residence during the week, spending weekends at home, when Stella pumped her about her studies, marks, friends and the like, while Noah pretended to read the *Leader and Recorder* or the *Mail and Empire*.

"Who is this Nathan you keep mentioning?" asked John Alex with an edge in his voice.

Jessica paused and chose to ignore the edge. "A friend of mine at Vic," she replied.

"A friend?"

"Yes, a friend, Nathan Fine. He has a fine mind and good ideas."

"A fine mind and good ideas. Nathan Fine has a fine mind and good ideas. Fine is fine. I get it."

"Look," she was reddening, "Can't you understand that university is about thought, and thinking and discussing ideas?"

"Go on."

"Nathan says, for instance, that the day of capitalism will pass, just as feudalism and slavery have passed. There is going to be a changed society; one in which men and women are equal, and workers will take over from owners, and we will produce cheaply what all the people need, instead of expensively what some of the people want. Workers will then have all the privileges that the rich have now."

"That sounds like a pipe dream to me."

"Johnny, I wish you could get some vision. What does it

say in the Bible? 'Where there is no vision, the people perish.'"

"It says a lot of things in the Bible. What religion is this Nathan?"

"Nathan is Jewish. He knows the Bible – at least, the Old Testament. He went to Hebrew school. I met him years ago when he helped Poppa on College Street after the pumper from the Fire Hall hit our car."

"I'll be…" muttered John Alex, as they turned up the walk to the lighted Oldfield veranda, and he remembered the black-bearded tailor who had told him of his son Nathan.

★　　★　　★

Some weeks later, Noah Oldfield came to Grogan's Diner and sat beside John Alex as he tackled a heaping plate of sausages, eggs and potatoes.

"What's happening with you and my daughter?"

"Nothing… Nothing. Why?"

"Nothing, eh! Don't joke with me, boy. She's been home every weekend. She was home for Easter. Didn't see you though."

John Alex looked down the counter to where Olga Grogan was drying a plate with her apron. Holding a skewered piece of sausage in midair – something Joanna Tyrone abominated – he waited until his mouth was empty.

"Jessica speak to you about us?"

"No, that's why I'm talking to you."

"Well, the fact is she isn't in my world anymore. I mean she's left where I am. I can't understand her language and her new friends."

"Damn! I thought as much. You give women a better

education and it goes straight to their heads."

"Well, not exactly. Most of the people in her special study groups are men. They don't all go to university, she told me. Sometimes, they meet at University Settlement House and listen to foreigners. Beats all."

Oldfield had a rough side, but he wasn't taken in by John Alex' explanation. He had seen, as Stella and the Fentons had seen, that John Alex was more than normally absorbed with Jessica – John Alex of the still waters whose jealousy took the form of polite removal, rather than confrontation.

This state of affairs couldn't be allowed to continue. It was endangering the most cherished dream of Oldfield's, which was to see his daughter – his only daughter – married to this handsome, intelligent, young man of good Anglican background and thus keep Royal Spring and Axle in the family, assuring its prosperity and the prosperity of his daughter. He was determined to make his dream a reality.

At supper, he tossed down his napkin beside his untouched dessert.

"Stella, there is something I've been wanting to ask."

"Yes."

"About Jessica and Johnny Tyrone."

"Yes."

"Do you notice that they are not seeing each other?"

"Yes, but I didn't think you had."

"I'm not blind. Johnny told me in Grogan's that Jessica has found some fancy friends at the university and he doesn't fit them anymore."

"That's rubbish! I'm as sure as you are that Jessica has a soft spot for Johnny."

"What can we do?"

54

"You don't want to be obvious."

"I'm listening…"

"Can't we organize a company picnic, maybe an excursion to Port Dalhousie. Invite the Fentons."

"An excursion? That will cost a sweet penny."

"Noah, I've discovered this about you — whenever you want to do something, you can come up with the money."

★   ★   ★

As it turned out, a catalytic circumstance stepped up the process. Jock Bain had a hand in this, without ever knowing.

Jock and his five-by-five squat wife Lassie kept a discrete bawdy house as an adjunct to their bootlegging business, which they started up after the Junction Ratepayers voted to close the taverns. Just a short stroll from Siding Street, this establishment sat behind some bushes next to a vacant lot, allowing drovers, road workers, shop mechanics and others to inconspicuously turn and slake their thirst or visit one of Jock's 'nieces'.

Since Jock and his wife could be sweet or formidable as circumstances dictated, most of their regular patrons paid up before leaving. Most anytime was the right time for stopping at Jock's, since either he or Lassie were available between nine in the morning and midnight. Frequently, one or more drovers, having completed an early cattle sale, would stop by Jock's for a drink, then go on to grab a coffee and sandwich at the Railway Restaurant on Siding Street before leaving town.

It was about ten on Monday morning when Olga Grogan came into Siding Street laden with bags of groceries. She had almost gained the steps into the diner when she heard a ruckus inside and a loud voice exclaiming, "Son of a bitch can't talk to me like that." Then the muddied figure and sunburnt face of a familiar drover, who frequently patronized Jock Bain's establishment, stumbled out into the street, knocking Olga into the picket fence and her groceries onto the ground. "Son of a bitch can't talk to me like that," said the sunburnt face again.

He faced Olga from about five feet as she straightened up and said, "Make tracks before I get the police." As she started to go up the steps, he moved with surprising agility, twirling her back onto the street where she lost her balance and fell.

"Whore!" he shouted, "Whore!"

"Mr. Tyrone, Mr. Tyrone," cried Miss Henty, "There's a disturbance down the street. Someone has knocked Mrs. Grogan down."

As John Alex came on the scene, Sunburnt said "Back off or I'll give you what I gave Grogan."

"Are you alright?" John Alex asked Olga. She nodded dazedly.

Torn between assisting Olga and checking on Grogan, he decided to assist Olga, without taking his eyes off Sunburnt, the drunk drover.

"Back off! Back off!" repeated Sunburnt, and as he said this, he ripped a loose picket from the fence and came for John Alex, who let him come within a few feet. Then, stepping to one side gave him a punch in the belly that toppled him to the road where he gasped and moaned without gaining his feet.

Inside the diner, they found Grogan holding his head in his hands and bleeding profusely from what proved later to be a broken nose.

It was a small enough incident, but it gained for John Alex some of the same respect on Siding Street that he had won in Humber Bend at MacSpadden's Highland Games.

★　★　★

They were on Lake Ontario, midway between Toronto and Port Dalhousie with the Royal Spring and Axle company excursion, when Jessica caught John Alex by the arm as he stood alone at the railing. He looked down at her, lovely as a rose at dawn in her summer taffeta, trying hard to suppress the pleasure he felt.

"Miss Henty told me you showed some mettle in assisting Mrs.Grogan. I'm proud of you."

"Are you? He asked.

"Yes. And don't you think it's time we ended this childish behaviour?" she said in a perfect imitation of Stella's brusque manner.

"I suppose so…"

"You suppose so," she mocked in a sing-song way. Then, looking deep into his eyes, she squeezed his arm and said, barely controlling her emotion, "I love you."

In a flash, his months of anger fell away. He took her by the waist, brought her tight to himself, and pressed a lingering kiss on her lips. He was totally unaware that other passengers were exchanging winks, or that Noah Oldfield was basking in one of Stella Oldfield's rare smiles.

It was a grand outing – the company excursion to Port Dalhousie. The strategem proposed by Stella had worked. Its main objective, that of Noah Oldfield to secure a worthy son-in-law and successor to take over Royal Spring, seemed hopeful again.

Shorty Cooper the machinist, unaware of the Oldfield's game, enjoyed his holiday greatly, helped no doubt by a twelve ouncer obtained from Jock Bain the night before – and his cantankerous wife's decision to stay home.

★   ★   ★

In November, Jessica and John Alex announced their engagement, delighting the Oldfields, Fentons and Mac-Larens who were called together for the occasion in the Oldfield's living room. To approving nods and smiles, the couple said the date for the wedding would be sometime after Jessica's graduation in May. Jimmy clapped his chubby hands when Stella turned to him and explained that this meant that John Alex and Jessica would now live in the same house together "like your father and I, and Mr. And Mrs. Fenton, and you can go and visit them."

John Alex took the news home at the end of the month, although Amy wrote to Joanna the day after the announcement. Joanna was elated: a woman with a university education could do much to further her son's career and advancement in the world.

But then, she had reservations. Doctors and lawyers and the clergy (the only university-educated people she knew) weren't prepared to be homemakers. Could she cook? Could she mend and sew? Could she press a shirt? These concerns were picked up by John Alex from her gentle allusions. He was not to be drawn, and when she remarked, "Watt is so fortunate to have a wife who can cook like Ella," he just let the implicit question hang and directed the conversation elsewhere. "Yes... Watt going to stand for reeve this year again?"

The simple truth is that Jessica had yet to consider domesticity in its conventional framework. Of one thing she was certain: the progressive, liberal attitude that she inherited from Stella and expanded in her university contacts would not evaporate when she became a Tyrone. She planned to gradually bring John Alex to the point where he could accept, and hopefully understand, this resolve on her part.

Certainly she loved him and believed unquestioningly in her ability to be a good and faithful wife. Being of a hopeful and naturally optimistic disposition, the question of carrying out her intentions within a marriage to one as conservative, staid and traditional as Johnny didn't faze her.

At Christmas, Jessica went with John Alex to Humber Bend. "Can't have them all the time to ourselves," Stella pointed out when Noah grumbled. Joanna and William Tyrone met them at the station with a sleigh. The women felt an immediate affinity for one another. Stolid William was beaming as they passed through the village, pulled at a trot by Queenie and Jack, their elegant driving team. It was a time of feasting and laughter in the house by the mill. Invited and uninvited guests kept dropping by to meet Jessica who was tickled by all the attention. John Alex couldn't wrest his eyes away from her radiance as she greeted each caller with a wide smile that revealed her good-humoured dimples and perfect teeth. It was a rare treat for the villagers to see the two smartly dressed women as they passed along Main Street, arm in arm, on Christmas Eve to do some last minute shopping at Walker's General Store.

As they passed by the blacksmith's on their way back, Angus McSpadden was just finishing a conversation with a pipe-smoking farmer about an infection in the foot of the farmer's mare. They tipped their hats to the women, who responded with warm smiles and "Merry Christmas". Angus nudged the farmer in the ribs, "Young Tyrone's got a beauty, I'd say." To which the farmer replied reflectively, exhaling a wreath of smoke into the sharp winter afternoon, "Yes, I'd say a beauty."

Christmas Eve at the house was a hubbub of last minute preparations suffused by the fragrance of baking, mingling with that of cold apples just brought up from the cellar. It was impossible for John Alex to get Jessica to himself privately, although he was burning with desire.

About nine-thirty, an hour which on other nights Humber Bend was in bed, Joseph McCaul knocked and let himself into the front hall.

"Just thought I'd drop around to wish you all the best of the season and to meet John Alexander's intended."

John Alex came up to him immediately and pumped his hand. "Mr. McCaul, good of you. We are just having a little Christmas cheer."

"Can't stay long Tyrone – sister down with the grippe. Ah, Miss Oldfield, delighted to meet you at last."

"That's mutual," said Jessica, "Johnny brings you into our conversation frequently."

"Will you join us in a glass of port and a little cake?" asked Joanna.

"Thanks, but no, Mrs. Tyrone, as I said, I have to get home. Mary Anne's running a fever… and Miss Oldfield, I *am* delighted to meet you, for word has it that you are the one who bested John Alexander in the provincial spelling champ-ionship a few years back." Jessica, blushing slightly, said, "It could have gone the other way, Mr. McCaul."

"Either way… That's a modest estimate, Miss Old-field…" He paused for a moment, then allowing himself a little smile, went on, "But, knowing your young man's spelling skill, I'd say there's some truth in it." He paused again, looking first at John Alex, then at Jessica, then at William and Joanna standing near the parlour door, he said, "Well yes, have to get along, sister sick as I said, but what I want to give the two of you young people for Christmas and as a wedding present to be remembered, is a little verse of Proverbs: *'Better is a dinner of herbs where love is, than a stalled ox and hatred therein.'*

"That's beautiful Mr. McCaul," said Jessica. "Johnny and I will value it always… *'Better is a dinner of herbs where love is…'*"

"*…than a stalled ox and hatred therein,*" chimed in John Alex.

McCaul gave the four of them a slight bow, put his bowler hat back on and reaching for the door said, "Good night, may the peace and joy of Christmas fill your hearts." As quickly as he'd come in, McCaul was gone again. "An interesting man," said Jessica. "Very," said John Alex, "has a knack for making you remember what he said."

The evening ended, as every Christmas Eve ended, with the Tyrones and Strabanes at the eleven o'clock eucharist in the Anglican church.

Before they left on the train on Boxing Day, Joanna had firmly decided, and conveyed to William and Watt, that, "Yes, this girl is the girl for Johnny – no question." The reservations she had had at the end of November had evaporated like the rum in her Christmas sauce.

Jessica cherished the memory of that Christmas in

Humber Bend for the rest of her days. The following May, she graduated from Victoria University and plunged into immigrant settlement work. The summer passed, and though she and John Alex talked frequently about wedding arrangements, an actual date wasn't set. When war with Germany came in August, he signed on, keeping his militia rank of sergeant in the Toronto Regiment.

"It'll be over in a matter of weeks or months and we have a lifetime ahead of us," he said. She didn't share his apparent optimism. Although, the possibility of a war had been predicted for some time, she felt cheated of something precious and anticipated. A little exasperated, he went on, "Well darling, have you nothing to say?" She paused, holding him, but looking away, thinking, and finally turning to face him directly. Her smile like a sunburst, she said, "Only this Johnny, neither land, nor sea, nor time can ever separate us."

The Oldfields and MacLarens saw him off at Union Station: Noah smiling; Stella clenching her parasol; Jimmy shouting, "Train, train!"

The Fenton twins were going on the same coach, having lied about their age to enlist. Walter, Joan and Robina were with them further along the platform.

John Alex solemnly shook hands with Noah, Stella, Jimmy and Don MacLaren. Amy clasped him to her bosom and whispered, "We will pray for you, Johnny. Come back."

Jessica stood before him, "I love you, Johnny."

"I love you too."

Over the din of commands, tramping feet and farewells, he barely heard her parting words, "I'll be writing often." He disappeared into the coach where the men were straining against one another to make their final farewells through the open windows. With a blast from its mighty steam lungs, the giant locomotive chuffed out of the station. At first, the crowd on the platform barely moved, then slowly it dispersed as from a funeral.

★   ★   ★

Robina Fenton was the female version of her husky brothers. Shortly after graduating from Humberside Collegiate with Jessica Oldfield, her best friend, she took a one-year business course at the Shaw Business College. Then, she immediately found employment with the Dodge Manufacturing Company. Vivacious, but sensible, she was described by the shipping department hands as "that blonde in the front office."

After two years with Dodge, she found a better position with the brokerage firm of Gunn-Lawson, as personal secretary to Roger Gunn. The firm was located on Adelaide Street, east of Bay, in the Empire building and occupied the entire third floor.

Roger Gunn was the majority shareholder and managing director having purchased Lawson's equity in 1909. R.G., as he was known by the other executives in the financial district, was a fierce competitor, an autocrat who always stood on his dignity.

Gunn's business and social dealings were with some of the most prominent promoters and financiers of the day – R.B. Bennett, Izaak Killam, Max Aitken, James Dunn and many others in Montreal, London, New York and Toronto. He was also careful to cultivate and reward a range of informants across the country and internationally, who were well placed to give him the latest information on prospects for investment in industry or promising mineral discoveries. He was among the first to plunge on Harry Oakes' Lakeshore Mine at Kirkland Lake, and the McIntyre Mine in Timmins.

It didn't pay to cross Roger Gunn. His grudges were many and his memory was long. He never tired of repeating "business is business", which meant he derived pleasure from his clients making money in the market, and took strong measures when they failed to pay their brokerage fees on time.

On her second day at Gunn-Lawson, Robina was called into Gunn's lavishly furnished office. He sat behind his desk, pince-nez on florid nose. The office was dominated by a large photograph of him turning the first sod of some development with a silver spade, while a clutch of prosperous types looked on.

"Take a letter, Miss Fenton."

"Yes sir."

"Mr. Peter Littlejohn – you'll find his address in the file."

"Yes sir."

"Sir, it's now over thirty days since you had this firm purchase 4000 shares of Spruce Gold on margin at 52 cents a share. That stock – Are you keeping up, Miss Fenton?"

"Yes sir."

"That stock dropped to fourteen cents a share by the close of trading yesterday. I advise you to place an immediate sell order and make a settlement of your obligation to us no later than the nineteenth of the month. Otherwise, we will be obliged to take action in the claims court. Yours truly, etc. etc."

"Will that be all, sir?"

"No, I have some other matters requiring personal attention. We will pick that up when I return from the Exchange. Meantime, have this letter to Littlejohn typed and ready for my signature. It's to go in the afternoon post."

Roger Gunn didn't meddle in the daily routine of the business, leaving that in the hands of J.O. Casey, his office manager. He only entered the main office to study the latest quotations on the ticker tape, or pass through on his way to the elevator.

Robina was stimulated by the frenetic atmosphere of the brokerage. Dodge Manufacturing was dull by comparison. The traders bouncing in and out were smartly dressed and wound up like coiled springs. When one of the mining stocks started to soar, there was a kind of controlled frenzy as orders to buy and sell tied up the phones. All the while, there was shouting from one desk to another for quotations and the never-ending backdrop of the ticker tape machine.

After trading closed at the exchanges in mid-afternoon, the pace at Gunn-Lawson slackened and the traders returned with their neckties askew to complete reports and records. This done, they quickly left for home or for Johnston's Billiard Hall on Temperance Street to do some convivial sipping in a back room. Roger Gunn departed for Rosedale shortly after in his chauffeur-driven sedan.

The men were delighted to have Robina on staff. The women less so, although she made the effort to be pleasant with everyone, including the stocky charwoman who, when the traders left, started her lonely clean-up of ticker tape and ash trays.

Gunn's only son Ned was brought into the firm after he graduated from Upper Canada College. In time, he was to be promoted to junior partner. As Gunn Senior explained to his confreres at the Albany Club, "I'm letting the boy learn the ropes, and the tricks of the trade from the ground up."

In the busy main office, it wasn't immediately obvious why Ned was so often at the water cooler. The exchange of bemused expressions finally indicated a general awareness that the boss's son was responding, not so much to thirst, as another normal urge. Robina, herself, finally tumbled. While he was, so he thought, innocently looking about, paper cup suspended, she caught him with her sky-blue eyes in an I'm-on-to-you way that flustered him. For a time, it ended his frequent thirst.

At noon the following day, as she was unwrapping her sandwich, Nancy Dalrymple leaned across the table.

"You have an admirer, I see."

"I guess so – it's a little uncomfortable."

"What are you going to do about it?"

"What *can* I do?"

"A lot of the girls would fancy a catch like Ned."

"It's crossed my mind. What's he like?"

"Rich. Good-looking. Never asked any of us out. Looks like he's about to start, if you don't scare him off."

That evening, Ned waylaid Robina just as she was about to pass through the heavy doors of the Empire Building onto Adelaide Street.

"Miss Fenton, may I have a word with you?"

"Yes, of course, can we step out onto the sidewalk? Please, call me Robina or Binny. I'd prefer that."

"And call me Ned or Neddy, that is what my mother calls me."

"I like Neddy, but I suppose men prefer Ned."

"Binny, I'm sorry about the water cooler."

"Forget it, please do."

Ned was stumped for an awkward moment, then got to what he wanted to ask. "Binny, the Annual Canoe Club Dance is on this Saturday. Will you be my date?"

"How very nice. Have to ask Poppa. Can I give you my answer tomorrow?"

"Heck, sure. Tell him I'll pick you up in my car and deliver you home before it turns into a pumpkin."

"Oh, you are droll. Does that suggest I'm Cinderella and you are Prince Charming?"

"That's stretching things. Let's say you are Princess Charming and I am your humble admirer."

All the long way home on the Dundas streetcar, Robina replayed the sidewalk experience in her mind. "He isn't a bear, like his father," she thought. "Handsome, nice smile… droll… rich. Jessica just has to hear about this." At the Junction, she stepped down from the back door onto the street and skipped the short distance home.

Ned arrived at the curb in front of the Fenton's at eight o'clock, as agreed. Walter and June Fenton came into the front room to be introduced. "Good-looking fellow," said Walter, after the couple departed. "Nicely mannered," said June. "Quite a car. Is that an Olds, Walter?"

"Yes, and from what Binny tells me, it's probably not the only one."

Ned took the long way to reach the Canoe, Club. In order to show off Robina, he wanted to arrive when most of the couples were already dancing, and in this he succeeded, for when they took to the floor in their first waltz, all eyes were on the radiant form of Robina Fenton. And then, as they glided about the floor, each delighted with the other's gaze, Ned forgot all about the attention they were drawing.

It was considered good form for a man to carry a hip flask on outings and Ned resorted to his a little too often during the evening. Driving home, he took a few corners wider than safety required. Emboldened by alcohol he moved his hand off the gear shift onto Robina's coat-covered thigh. She swiftly and firmly lifted it back to the gear shift. "You know, Mr. Ned," she said, with emphasis on *Mister*, "we Fentons are not wealthy, nor prominent – neither are we fools. For your information, Momma told me that a hat pin can have its uses when a young lady is out with a gentleman."

He studied the street ahead for a full minute. "Sorry," he finally mumbled in a subdued way, "some girls don't seem to mind."

To which she replied, "I'm not *some girls*."

On Monday, Ned kept to his end of the office, feeling sheepish about Saturday night and miffed that the most fetching young woman of his limited experience wasn't bowled over by him. Robina studiously ignored him for a few days, even when he started to drift over to the water cooler with increasing frequency. If he knew anything about the little game in the main office, Roger Gunn didn't let on and at some point, Robina began to suspect that he wasn't even aware that Ned had dated her.

After a week of this charade, Ned caught up to Robina as she stepped briskly along Adelaide to catch the Bay streetcar.

"And how is young Mr. Gunn today?" she asked pleasantly.

"Fine, just fine, I was wondering, Binny…"

"Wondering – as in when you can date me again. Am I correct?"

"Yes, absolutely correct. In fact, I haven't been thinking of much else lately. I was wondering, if it's nice on Sunday afternoon, could we go walking out your way?"

Her smile was all the affirmative he required, and they parted.

The Sunday afternoon in rich autumn colours, was most pleasurable – followed by other Sunday afternoon strolls until plunging temperatures forced them into heavier clothing and a brisker pace. By mid-December, the affair looked like more than a passing fancy to June Fenton, and Ned was invited to Sunday dinner. A few weeks later, Robina received an invitation to dinner at the Gunn's on Charlotte Gunn's monogrammed vellum stationary.

★   ★   ★

Power meant more to Roger Gunn than ostentation, yet when Ned and Robina drove through the gate of the Gunn mansion in Rosedale, Robina gasped at the scale of the place with its high portico and vaulted conservatory.

At dinner, Roger and Charlotte Gunn sat at the head and foot of the table. Ned and Robina sat on one side and Charlotte's brother Sir John Clark and his wife Lady Clark sat on the other. Sir John was simply Jack or Uncle Jack in the family. He had been put on the King's honour list by the Borden cabinet in recognition of his many philanthropies, including that of the Conservative Party.

Lady Clark had been an internationally recognized mezzo-soprano – Marie LaRoque – often feted in London and New York. She was pursued by John Clark in both cities

– before he was knighted. They married in the summer of 1908.

In October, while riding in Central Park, she was thrown from her horse. This left her with a permanently painful back, the loss of her operatic career, and a chronically sour disposition.

Soup was served by Norton the butler. Roger Gunn muttered a hardly audible table grace. The meal commenced in silence.

Between courses, Lady Clark looked across at Robina. "Miss Fenton, Neddy tells me you play the pianoforte, is that so? No doubt, at least a few two-step tunes – by ear perhaps?"

"Yes, I studied piano at the Toronto Junction College of Music, but stopped when I went to business college."

"How interesting. It would never occur to me that the daughter of a working man would ever take up music or the arts. Most remarkable. Don't you agree, Charlotte?"

Ned cleared his throat as though starting to say something, but with a flush of pink rising from her neck, Robina looked across the table and in an even tone said, "Oh, not remarkable at all Lady Clark. I'm sure you are familiar with the names of Enrico Caruso, Richard Wagner and others with working-class roots. And, of course, there are many poets and painters whose names may not be familiar to you in the artistic world…"

Lady Clark's eyes lowered. Sir John muttered, "Just so, just so." The maid cleared away the soup plates. Norton arrived with the roast duck.

Hoping to retrieve the evening from its downward slide, Ned said, "Tell us again Uncle Jack about the time you pulled the wool over the eyes of those militia buyers."

"You've heard that before, Ned. Did I ever tell you of how I got my start with the Lucky Jack Mine?"

"Perhaps," interjected Charlotte, "you would prefer to tell us that humourous story of the time you had tea with the Asquiths in London and Lady Asquith's cat jumped on the table."

"Naw," said Sir John, feeling the effect of his third glass of wine, "a red-blooded boy like Ned doesn't want to hear stuff like that."

"Oh, if you must," said Charlotte, looking apprehensively at Robina, who was beginning to relax and enjoy herself.

"Go ahead, Jack," grunted Roger Gunn.

"Well, long before I ever met Marie, I headed for the Yukon from Seattle in '98. Made a tiny little profit at cards before we reached Skagway. The second night in Dawson, I went to the Deuces Wild Saloon and here were some of the same Americans I played with on the trip down north and a few sourdoughs who had made a strike. That was some night, I'm telling you Ned, the whiskey was flowing like water."

Charlotte cut in, "Watch what you say, Jack, you are in the presence of ladies."

"Well, I nearly went under a couple of times," Sir John continued, "but managed to come back. Do you believe in luck, Ned? I do. The game seesawed until there were only four of us, and then three, and then just Montana Red – didn't know him by any other name – and myself. I put everything I had in the centre of the table and drew a full house against Montana Red's three of a kind. We played right through the midnight sun until it was four in the morning.

From that day, I was known as Lucky Jack, and when I

took control of the Lynx Mine on Bonanza Creek, I renamed it Lucky Jack. Stayed in Dawson for a year and never had to put a spade in the ground myself."

"Well, there you have it," growled Roger Gunn, "You got a start like a lot of the rest of the swells selling stocks and swindles on Bay Street."

"Uncle Jack, that's a wonderful story, I hope I can have your good luck," said Ned. His father was not amused. "You'll stay away from cards and drink if you know what's good for you. Dammit Jack, don't you see that for every gambler like you, there's a thousand ruined?"

"That I don't deny," said Sir John, "I long ago moved my gambling from the card table to the stock exchange. Mind you, I do like the horses."

It was Lady Clark's turn to blush, something Roger Gunn detected with pleasure. He had never liked her from the first day they met, a sentiment that only deepened when, through one of his New York agents, he discovered that her birth name was Myrtle Fraily and her father had been a Brooklyn brick layer.

Had the dinner proceeded otherwise, Robina might have been asked to play in the drawing room as Norton served coffee, but Sir John's reminiscence hadn't really lifted the pall spread by his mate, and Charlotte didn't want to add insult to Lady Clark's comeuppance. The only bit of cheer seemed to come from the giant hearth where a crackling fire sent its heat and light into the circle of six people straining to understand the significance of this ill-fated soiree.

Finally, Charlotte said, "Neddy, perhaps Miss Fenton would enjoy a little tour of the conservatory and the library."

"Great idea," said Ned.

"And perhaps you men would like to take your cigars up to the billiard room. I want to discuss our New Year's celebration with Marie."

Upstairs, as they were removing their jackets and lighting their cigars, Roger Gunn squinted at Sir John and asked, "What do you think a good buy might be on Wall Street, Jack?"

"Oil."

"Hmm, oil, eh?"

"Yes, oil — and steel."

"Rockefeller and Carnegie, eh?"

"Yes, something like that."

Why? Haven't they been flat lately?"

"It's just a feeling R.G., maybe nothing more, but a number of investors are betting there could be a war. Probably between France and Germany, maybe pull in Britain, and if there is, American steel and oil will be in demand. Just the speculation is bound to drive prices up. You'll want to get in before the preferred stock is grabbed by people like Baruch."

"Damn Jew. Why do we allow people like that to get where they do?"

"I guess you could call it democracy, R.G. . . . How long do you think you're going to be able to keep Jews from getting seats on the exchanges up here."

"Damned if I know. But these people who put you up for a knighthood should lower the boom on immigration except for white men."

"Okay, okay, R.G. . . . Oil and steel. Don't say I didn't tell you." Sir John, who was a man of the world in a way that his brother-in-law could never be, was nettled by the turn in the

73

discussion. He chalked his cue, struck the cue ball and said, "Five will get you ten, if you can carom with what I've left you."

Some time later, Roger Gunn and Sir John Clark descended to the drawing room – the former put out of sorts by his losses to the latter. "It's getting on," said Sir John consulting his watch. "Come dear, we must make for the King Edward. Remember, this is Toronto and they roll up the streets at midnight."

In the front hall, after Norton had handed them their things, Sir John said, "Thanks for the evening. Say good night to the young people for us. Handsome pair. Wouldn't you agree, dear?" With a wink to his brother-in-law, Sir John took his wife's arm and walked through the door towards their car.

After the Clarks exited, Roger Gunn queried Charlotte on the whereabouts of the young couple. She replied that they were in the library or possibly the conservatory, and wasn't it time that Miss Fenton was taken home.

The lights were dimmed low when Gunn stepped into the library, but still there was enough light for him to see Ned and Robina stretched out in an embrace on the sofa at the end of the room. Without comment, he cleared his throat authoritatively and went back out.

Later as the hall clock chimed twelve and the Gunns were getting into bed, Roger said to Charlotte, "We have to get this affair between Ned and Miss Fenton into gear." To which Charlotte replied, "Whatever do you mean?"

"I mean we have to get them married."

"Married, oh dear, has anything happened that I haven't been told?"

"Not yet that I'm aware, But it's what can happen that

concerns me. An ounce of prevention is worth a pound of cure. Found them sparking full length on the library sofa."

"Well… but Robina… Miss Fenton… she really isn't our sort… very modest means. Her father is only an hourly-rated mechanic. Heaven knows what her mother is like. They're hardly people of any social standing.

"Poppycock, Charlotte, poppycock. You're forgetting how we started out with hardly a plug nickel between us. Fact is this girl has brains and beauty. I've had plenty of opportunity to observe her. Very quick. Very intelligent. Can stand up for herself, and Ned if need be. Did you see how she handled our Miss Oh-so-fancy LaRoque?"

"There's no call to be sarcastic, Roger. But, you are right."

"My mind is made up. We should strike while the iron is hot, and it is hot, believe me."

In the morning, Roger caught Ned in the vestibule as he was leaving for work − always 45 minutes ahead of his father.

"Just a minute, my buck."

"Yes, father?"

"You have strong feelings for Miss Fenton?"

"Yes, father − very."

"Do you think she can make a good helpmate − a good wife?"

"Yes, father."

"Well then, propose to her and be damn quick about it, before you get yourselves and us into trouble. Do you take my meaning?"

"Yes, father, I'll do that. I want to do that. I won't delay, believe me."

The fact of the proposal didn't come as so much of a surprise to Robina, as did the timing. But, on canvassing her emotions and the benefits that such a liaison could confer on herself and her family, she agreed to be Ned's wife on the condition that both of her parents consented. They did, and very quickly the date was arranged for the third Saturday in May, three months before the outbreak of war.

Victoria Presbyterian Church in the Junction had rarely, if ever, seated such a distinguished company for a wedding. Sir John Clark stood beside Ned, and Jessica Oldfield beside Robina.

A few days later, the Mail and Empire's social column described the occasion:

> The wedding on Saturday of Mr. Edward Justyn Gunn of Rosedale and Miss Robina Fenton of West Toronto was a highlight in this year's social calendar. The groom is the only son of Mr. and Mrs. Roger Gunn, and is with his father's firm Gunn-Lawson Brokerage. The bride is the only daughter of Mr. and Mrs. Walter Fenton of West Toronto Junction. Victoria Presbyterian Church on Annette Street was the setting for the beautiful nuptials presided over by the Reverend Doctor Naismith Macmurdo. Sir John Clark, brother of the groom's mother, was best man and Miss Jessica Oldfield was Maid of Honour. Miss Anne Storey sang two selections from Handel's Sampson and Delilah. Among the distinguished guests were Their Excellencies John Morrison Gibson and Mrs. Gibson, the Honourable James Whitney and Mrs. Whitney, Sir Joseph and Lady Flavelle, and Lady Clark former mezzo-soprano with the Metropolitan Opera of New York. After the ceremony, family and guests

departed for the Eglinton Hunt Club and then onto the King Edward Hotel for dinner and dancing. The newly-weds left the affair early to catch the late train for New York City. They will be away on an extended honey-moon in the United States and Europe.

While Ned and Robina were still honeymooning in Europe, Roger Gunn purchased a house for them in Moore Park, quite modest by Rosedale standards, yet roomy enough with a maid's room on the first floor. They were barely back, still shopping for furniture, when war broke out.

Ned volunteered, a matter of course for Upper Canada College old boy and scion of the Anglo establishment. In late September, he became a second lieutenant in the Toronto Scottish Regiment and in a few days followed his brothers-in-law and John Alex Tyrone to Valcartier in Quebec for training.

He met Frank and Stanley just once, on the road running between their regimental lines, and the twins found the business of saluting their one pip brother-in-law highly amusing. A few days before his regiment embarked for England, Ned ruptured himself helping to push a gun carriage. He was hospitalized, returned to Toronto, and discharged.

★   ★   ★

The war barely fazed the business at Gunn-Lawson. The traders who enlisted were quickly replaced by others from competing firms. The volume of trading in industrial stocks and base metals increased, but was manageable. Things were pretty much on an even keel.

Roger Gunn looked forward to moving greater

77

responsibility onto Ned's shoulders, who after his army discharge, moved back to the firm. After a short meeting with his office manager, J.O. Casey, the carpenters were called in to partition an office between his own and Casey's for Ned. Below the frosted pane of the new office door, a brass plate declared: "E.J. Gunn, Assistant to the President". It was Roger Gunn's intention that in time, the plate would read: "Vice President"; and then "President".

Ned had to spend considerable time in the exchanges, both the Standard Stock and Mining Exchange, and the Toronto Stock Exchange. Then, much to his chagrin, he was compelled to stay after the staff and his father left for the day putting memoranda reports into the Dictaphone for his secretary, Nancy Dalrymple, to retrieve in the morning.

At first, as a kind of democratic gesture, he would cross over to Johnston's Billiard Hall when he had finished, sharing in a convivial round with whoever was still around from Gunn-Lawson or other nearby brokerages. With the passing of time, he found this practice more and more to his liking. Frequently, his supper was cold by the time he reached home and an exasperated Robina was not to be placated by feeble apologies and attempts at endearment.

★   ★   ★

The grisly cast of the war began to hit home in the spring of '15. Robina and her parents were devastated by the twins' deaths at Ypres. The news put much of West Toronto in shock. Jessica did everything she could to comfort the Fentons, spending hours with them. The principal of Humberside Collegiate declared a day of mourning, the first of many, and closed classes at noon. The lacrosse team filled a long pew in the Victoria Presbyterian Church for a special memorial service.

On July 6, the thermometer registered over 90 degrees for a third consecutive day. Roger Gunn had just gone down the elevator and Ned, with the thought of a whet at Johnston's foremost on his mind, was sorting through the results of the day's trading in his shirt sleeves beside the open window. An angry voice rose from the hot street, "You have this coming to you, you bastard!"

There were two shots in rapid succession. From the third floor window, Ned looked down to see his father slumped into the back seat of his car, legs akimbo over the running board. The chauffeur stood frozen, holding the handle of the door he had seconds before opened for his employer.

The murderer made no effort to get away, but stood beside the brass front door of the building, revolver still in hand pointed at the sidewalk. Ned came down the back stairs on the run and bolted out onto the sidewalk. "Jesus Christ! What have you done?" he shouted at him.

"Call the police, your old man had it coming" was the reply.

Next day, the papers played up the murder. Under a front page headline in the Toronto Daily Star, a report was lavishly supplemented by pictures of Roger and Charlotte Gunn at the running of the Queen's Plate in 1912; of Gunn in blood-stained tropical suit stretched across the car's running board; and of police leading away a hand-cuffed man identified in the caption as Peter Littlejohn of Parkdale, prime suspect in the murder.

According to the Star,

Roger Gunn, president of Gunn-Lawson Broker-age, was murdered yesterday at approximately 6 p.m. outside his Adelaide Street office. The alleged culprit, one Peter Littlejohn, made no attempt to escape the scene of the crime and was found by police with the alleged murder weapon, a partially loaded repeater, still in hand. City Coroner Dr. C.L. James said the victim died instantaneously with massive brain injury and arterial hemorrhaging. It appears that there were two shots at point blank range, one entering the head and the other the upper torso.

Informed sources in the financial district hint that Littlejohn had for some time been over-extended in risky stock ventures. J.O. Casey, office manager at Gunn-Lawson, informed this reporter that the firm has been trying for some time to collect Littlejohn's arrears. Casey overheard an angry exchange just last week between Gunn and Littlejohn in the former's office. Littlejohn is being held at the Don Jail and a preliminary hearing is expected early next week at City Hall.

While not yet confirmed, it is expected that E.J. Gunn will now assume the presidency of his late father at Gunn-Lawson. Located this morning at his parents' Rosedale home, Gunn would only comment on the deep shock and grief of the family. He did add that his uncle, the Montreal financier Sir John Clark, would arrive this evening by train from Montreal.

The body of the late Roger Gunn will repose in Rosedale until Friday at noon, when it will be transferred to St. Andrew's Presbyterian Church on King Street for the funeral."

John Alex suspected — rightly as it turned out — that the injury to his knee would leave him with a permanent problem. The tone of the doctors, when they pronounced the necessity for a lengthy convalescence, confirmed his suspicion.

The wound was a trap, would be a trap, always — but an honourable thing, he mused. If he had any resentment, it was directed at those who, in his opinion, hadn't seen their duty as clearly as he had. The slackers. The laggards. The shirkers. Those who hadn't and wouldn't do their bit without being driven to it.

Still, he was gripped by a sense of guilt. It was there at dawn when he awakened. He was haunted by the Fenton boys, chopped into the mud only a few yards apart in the enfilade at St. Julien — consumed by the voracious maw of hell. Why them? Why not him?

Yet, he was grateful, oh so grateful, to be out of the Minotaur's labyrinth that was Flander's — out of the ear-splitting noise of the bombardment, out of the grasp of constant fear, out of the stench of rotting flesh, out of the pervasive cold and dampness. And to be held — amazingly — at Queen's Hill alive, safe and in a clean dry bed.

It was grimly amusing, this being alive — filled with irony. He had been as good as dead in No Man's Land, and the hand that saved him was a bullet in the knee, instead of the heart. There had been no such hand for Frank and Stanley.

Much more came to his mind in that dawn hour: Joseph McCaul, standing by the blackboard, dark jacket immaculately brushed, high collar jutting into his chops, holding a dog-eared Bible during morning exercises:

From the blood of the slain
from the fat of the mighty
the bow of Jonathan turned not back,
and the sword of Saul returned not empty.
Saul and Jonathan, beloved and lovely!
In life and in death, they were not divided;
they were swifter than eagles,
they were stronger than lions.
How are the mighty fallen
in the midst of the battle!

In a trice, his thought shifted from Humber Bend School to the straw-covered courtyard at Mouse Trap Farm, where he was lying in a litter when word came back about the Fenton boys. "How are the mighty fallen," he cried out, shaking up the ward.

"Are you alright, Captain?"

"Yes Sister, I'm alright... sorry."

And even as he said this, he was thinking of a long summer dusk spent on Oldfield's veranda, as Frank and Stanley ran home from a lacrosse game twirling their sticks, bouncing and whipping the ball to one another – laughing all the while.

★   ★   ★

The British officers in the ward were civil, but cool with their Canadian counterparts. Despite his own reserve, John Alex was used to a warmer camaraderie. Over a game of cribbage, he raised the matter with a fellow Canadian, Lieutenant Archie McLean. Gassed at the front, McLean's breathing was torturous, his talk punctuated with coughs.

"Yes – well interesting these English officers... a-khoo... a-khoo... a-khoo... damn!"

"How so?"

"They're right as rain, you know... uh-huh... courageous..."

"Courageous, yes... and arrogant, yes!"

"Not with their own... a-khoo... damn... not with their own... but they have a silly notion... a-khoo... but they have a silly notion that they belong to a superior breed. Indeed, some of them have a pedigree – uh-khoo... went to Oxford... Sandhurst... great-great-grandfather fought with Wellington."

"So what. For all I know, my great-great-grandfather fought with Wellington."

Yes. Perhaps – uhummm – maybe mine did too. Point is were they commissioned gentlemen who returned to estates and servants. Were they connected gentry? Did they – uh-khoo – did they marry into people of social rank?"

"To hell with all of that!"

"Yes, but it is bred in the bone with them to think differently. All... all... uh-khoo... all their lives they have been taught that they are not only part of the nation set apart... uh-koom... but a social class set apart... they... a-khoo... damn!... they know that you and I were raised from the ranks, we were not born to the officer class, or if you prefer, the gentleman class... they truly see themselves as the modern equivalent of Plato's guardians or Roman patricians... to them we are like a wild card in the pack... colonial... allies in the war... but still outside the pale."

"Archie, I'll tell you something. This war might last and

the English are going to learn that they haven't an edge on the colonials... Sir Sam Hughes can stand up to the best they have."

"Uh-kuh-h-h... uh-kuh... damn...I think so myself. The whole class system over here is going to come down like a house of cards. But do you realize that much more is at stake? Imperialism itself will shoot its bolt with the war, and that is what has buttressed this English class arrangement for so long..."

"You're not getting into socialism, are you Archie? I've no use for socialists. Came across some in Toronto. No use."

Time will tell about that," dissembled Archie, "but we need to look at ourselves – uh-humm."

"Need to look at ourselves?"

"Matter of consistency. Fairness. We don't like this snooty Britishness – then what about us...?"

"What about us?"

"What I have in mind – uh-kuh-humm... is to me worse than class snobbery. Too many of our kind back home want to give the boot to immigrants... no Russian, German, Pole... kick them out... kick out the Jews. Save the country for Jones and Smith, Tyrone and McLean. Ever hear talk like that? Tell me, what makes us so God Almighty superior? Why... uh-kuh... why the English officers are absolutely civilized with us by comparison..."

"You know, Archie, you sound just like my fiancee Jessica. I'll have to chew this over. Well, time to eat, same.old bully beef, I suppose. Can't wait to get back to Toronto... sit at my sister Amy's table again."

★　　★　　★

Until he was shipped to Flanders, a regular flow of letters reached John Alex from England. At Christmas in Bustard Camp, he received almost indentically wrapped packages from Jessica, Amy and Joanna... socks from Amy, mitts from Joanna (she had always knit superior ones for the Tyrone and Strabane men), and a huge muffler from Jessica monogrammed JAT in a circle above the tassles on each side.

He kept the muffler in his kit, and then lost it forever when he lost everything at Mouse Trap Farm. In convalescence, he mused that he lost his scarf but saved his precious life!

For whatever reason, and there could have been many, he didn't get mail from home for five months. Then, a bundle of letters bound with twine found him on October 22. It was a letter from Jessica dated September 12 that gave him the greatest pleasure:

Dear Johnny,

I hardly know where to start, but first you should know that Robina is still horribly distressed, as are her parents, over the loss of Stanley and Frank. It's hit this household hard too — Momma and Poppa couldn't have thought more of those boys had they been their own. We know you have to be devastated as well, Johnny. We have kept the news from Jimmy.

Robina's grief was compounded in July, when Roger Gunn was murdered on the street below his office in broad daylight. Mrs. Gunn is bearing up, but you can see that there's a pall over that house. Ned's drinking doesn't help. Enough. Now, maybe this will brighten you up. I hope to see you in England before Spring arrives. My application for the Voluntary Aid Detachment, or

VAD, is being considered as I write (I hope)! Poppa is paying my passage to England, where I can enlist with them. It's all been arranged through one of Poppa's suppliers, who has family in London. Poppa didn't take to the idea at first, but Momma leaned on him. The VADs help as general factotums in hospitals. Poppa is busy – has more orders than he can handle and I've been going in most days to help in the office. I hope you won't be offended to learn that I've been doing a bit of your old job. Jimmy keeps asking for you, and guess what, Poppa finally broke down and got him a dog. It's just a puppy, but his mother is a beautiful collie. Our name for him is Jack. It was Jimmy's choice, since Fenton's dog that died last year was named Jock.

Too-da-loo, Fentons are coming for dinner and I must help Momma.

Oceans of Love, Always Yours,

Jessica

A clipping of the Roger Gunn murder coverage was folded into Jessica's letter. He'd only met Roger Gunn perfunctorily as a guest at Robina and Ned's wedding. Even though he'd been surrounded by death at the Front, the wanton murder of the vital personality touched him.

Her letter, despite the background of heaviness, lifted his spirits, almost making him break forth in song. A nursing sister going by with a bedpan caught the animation in his expression. "Good news, Captain, is it? You look like the. cat that swallowed the canary." Through the remainder of the dark autumn day, he ran and re-ran those magic words across the screen of his mind: *hope to see you in England before Spring arrives.*

The letter aroused in him a warmth of desire that took his thoughts back to the rail of the Dalhousie excursion boat. After the ward lights went down, he continued to think of her, and falling asleep with her letter still in his hand, he dreamt that they kissed, drawing close to one another.

After breakfast, an orderly or nursing sister would take him into the garden. His cast-bound leg projecting forward, required that every turn be negotiated with care. It would be some time before movement of the knee could be tested, or the weight of his body placed upon two legs again.

Never a keen reader, he also found small talk difficult. Despite Jessica's bright communication, he lapsed easily into a gloomy mind-set. Under the strict measures of the Defence of the Realm Act, it was forbidden to talk or publish in defeatist terms. But, that aside, most of the civilian and military population preferred to believe that it was just a question of time for the 'big push' to be made — a matter of a few months at the most — and the allies would emerge victorious.

Having experienced the fury of the Ypres Salient and the earth-shuddering impacts of the German 'Big Berthas', John Alex suspected otherwise. It was dawning on him that the war was the product of something that had gone deeply sour, not only in Germany or the Austro-Hungarian Empire, but with all of the war's protagonists — with so-called civilizations that could send youth into war's madness. Yes, the Boche had to be stopped. Couldn't have them trampling over Belgium and breaking treaties. What had got into them in the first place? Still...

His thoughts went back to an evening when he and Jessica were sipping cocoa in the Oldfield's kitchen after bobsledding in High Park, toes and finger-tips still tingling form the cold. Then, out of nowhere, Jessica said, "Nathan believes that the industrialists and bankers want war. Why? Good for productivity, profits and imperial expansion, that's why. They welcomed the South African war for that very same reason, he says."

His ire rose at this out-of-the-blue remark. "That may be or not. I don't know. I know that Talwyn Smythe, the accountant over at the Bank of Toronto, is one of the finest men I know."

"You are impossible," she said with a smile.

Now, he began to think Nathan made sense. He was getting bloody tired of the jingoism... The padre on Sunday morning: "Let us pray for all the gallant chaps, yourselves included, officers and men who have been willing to make the supreme sacrifice for motherland, freedom and democracy"... Milly the charwoman: "If I 'ad old Kaiser Bill 'ere, I'd put 'is 'ead in this 'ere bucket, I would"... The scribble on the wall of the loo: "Oh what a day, when jerry's flushed away"...

For some days, Jessica's letter eased his gloom, but then he felt it gradually taking over again. He struggled to overcome it by a conscious act of will.

He summoned into memory, the sun-brushed summer hills of his childhood; the Humber's quiet flow between chickory-lined banks; the Strabane clydes standing head-to-rump in the shade of an elm, flicking away flies with their great tails, shaking their manes, and giving little snorts as they trotted tandem down their old path to drink in the river; himself, naked and alone, stretched in the shallows under the bank with the gentle water caressing him; and Jessica, who had never been to Humber Bend in the summer, came into the scene.

This benediction would have been incomplete without her. Thus, he imagined them sitting in the shade of the bridge on the river's bank, and the fragrance of her hair went out to him.

Still, the horror of Ypres would push back – couldn't be suppressed – a hellish scene of men and horses entangled in barb wire, ripped apart by gunfire, bleeding, choking to death, face-down in the cold mud.

How could the pastoral bliss of Humber Bend co-exist in this world with the reality of war in Flanders? Wasn't Flanders, too, once a place of pastoral beauty and peace? Maybe – and this was a comforting thought – maybe the juxtaposition lay behind the allied resistance, and the contagion of hell was being stopped before it spread.

Hell? Mrs. Minty had wagged her finger at Watt when she found him puffing on a cigar one Sunday. Didn't he realize he was in danger of going to hell?? "Young man, you should be reading your Bible, instead of destroying the temple of the Holy Spirit with that thing on the Lord's Day." Would Mrs. Minty ever know, he wondered, of the actual hell, the hell on earth, that hell which the sons of tens of thousands of mothers like herself, were enduring in Flanders?

The grey autumn wore on without further word from Jessica and it was a greyer day than usual in November – a sodden mist-filled day that hung like a wraith over Queen's Hill; a day of damp and cold in the dim wards; a day, thought John Alex, that suited the sadness of his own spirit.

There was a similar day in Humber Bend, he remembered, when he looked through the rain-flecked windows of the school into the grey of Mrs. Warminster's pasture and onto her three Jersey cows standing transfixed to the sod in their wet hides.

"Attention class. You, Tyrone, eyes to the front."

Joseph McCaul detested slackness in his class. "The soul – that part of us that is eternal; that invisibly houses our fondest instincts; is often influenced by the seasons and the weather. Poets sometimes use the weather as a metaphor for our moods. On a day like today, we don't feel as bright as we do on a summer day. You can say that today is a melancholy day – remember that word melancholy meaning dismal, gloomy, or sad. I want the senior class to memorize these lines by William Cullen Bryant."

And here, John Alex remembered McCaul going to the blackboard and effortlessly writing in a flowing script:

The melancholy days are come,
the saddest of the year,
of wailing winds, and naked woods,
and meadows brown and sere.

"Melancholy days? Too many melancholy days over here," the captain with the smashed knee muttered. "I'd trade this place in summer for any melancholy November day in Humber Bend – any melancholy day in January by the fire with Jessica."

Half awake, he heard a voice above him. "Miss to see you, sir, in the conservatory." The orderly handed him a calling card:

Jessica Oldfield, B.A.
Voluntary Aid Detachment,
35B Farrington Road, London

The moment the orderly pushed him into the conservatory, she was beside him and planting a kiss on his cheek.

"Johnny, you look thin. When can they get that awful thing off? You get my letter?"

His eyes misted over. "Great balls of fire!" was all that he could blurt out and his arm went instinctively around her slim waist.

"Is that all you have to say?" she said, "Do you like my card?"

He was regaining his composure. "Sure, I like your card. When did you get to London? I did get your letter, by the way, saying you were coming."

"A week ago. Couldn't get away until now and wanted to surprise you."

"And what a wonderful surprise it is. I see some sunshine breaking through my cloudy days."

"I told you, in the letter, about the VADs, Johnny."

"Yes. Where are you putting up?"

"That's what it tells you in my card, silly... 35B Farrington Road. It's a hospice called St. Luke's, run by Anglican nuns that's been changed over to a small military hospital. I live in the same building with some other VADs, mostly old country, but there's one other Canadian. I'm learning in a hurry about the ugliness of war."

★   ★   ★

In December, Jessica wrote home:

Arrived safely... seasick a lot... Johnny ,in a wheelchair, hip to ankle cast... we hope to be together at Christmas... this is a small hospital nursing wounded from France... I'm taking more classes with the St. John's Ambulance.

She didn't try to convey the impact of her hours in St. Luke's wards. Couldn't. The horrible wounds and mutilations. The reek of pus and feces that hung in the air and in her clothes. Or the kick in the shin she gave an intern who made a pass at her in the stairwell.

As it turned out, she wasn't able to go down to Queen's Hill until New Year's Eve. She found John Alex finishing his noon meal of herring and boiled potatoes.

"You eat like a horse, Johnny."

"Yes, and I'm looking forward to the day when I can buck and prance like one, too."

"I like that... bucking..." There was a twinkle in her eye.

The fire of their passion was consuming them. As dusk fell in the conservatory, she stood beside his chair and let him slide his hand down over the camber of her hip, while they basked in tenderness.

Some time elapsed and then, tussling his hair, she said, "As soon as you get that leg down on the floor and you're walking again, we're going to get married. It's silly to wait 'til we're back home." He nodded – smiling broadly – but before he could speak, she went on. "Momma and Poppa will understand. They are as anxious to have us married as we are." She threw her head back in an affirmative way that, just for a moment, made him think of his mother.

★   ★   ★

The other Canadian VAD at St. Luke's was Helen Church of Halifax. She and Jessica saw a lot of each other. In their limited free time, they visited a few of London's famous places: evensong at St. Paul's Cathedral; the British Museum

(because before leaving Toronto, Jessica met Nathan at St. Christopher House and he said, "You have to visit the British Museum. It's a shrine. Marx produced *Das Kapital* in there.")

Jessica had to push to keep up with Helen's quick walking pace. Coming out of Madame Tussaud's, Jessica said, "That was interesting, but frankly, we are seeing enough horror right in these streets and St. Luke's. Hardly need reminding of those poor souls decapitated in the French Revolution."

"Yes, but the whole thing is a tribute to what a woman has done with her talent. We need to see and hear more of what women can do in this world."

"I agree. You're right. Though my beau requires some enlightening. Tell me, at Dalhousie, did you have a women's rights group?"

"Yes. You will be interested to know that a group of women at Dal wanted to sponsor me to the Women's International League for Peace and Freedom in The Hague. Had to decline – already committed to the VAD."

"Can we put our VAD experience into the women's movement?"

"Absolutely. Women are on the move. A lot is happening here in England, right under our noses."

"Say on."

"Work. Dress. Roles. Freedoms. Right here! Right here in England."

"You mean land-girls. Men's pants. Bus conductorettes. Munitionettes. Short dresses?"

"All that – all that and women still don't have the vote."

"Surely, that's coming."

"It is, and soon. Still a lot of stick-in-the-mud men will do what they can to slow the advance. Before coming over, I had a visit with the editor at the Halifax Morning Herald. Now, there is a typical male reactionary telling me women aren't content anymore with hearth and home – his very words. Gave me a copy of the Times in which Asquith is reported as requesting Emmeline Pankhurst to suspend her suffrage agitation for the sake of the war effort."

"And, what did you say to him?"

"Not much, I'm afraid. I got in to see him because I was coming over here and I wanted him to let me file some articles on women in the war effort."

"Go on."

"He hummed and hawed and said to come in the next day after he discussed it with staff. Which I did, and he said they had no examples of my writing, but if I'd like to file a weekly or bi-weekly article of two or three hundred words, they would print under the heading *Women at War*. He offered a straight ten dollars per article.

"And, have you got started?"

"Yes, I've already sent an article on VAD – the kinds of things we are doing in the hospitals. Have to be very circumspect."

That night, Jessica was exhausted. With a heavy period, she should have refused Helen's invitation to visit Tussaud's. It was barely dark when she excused herself from the little parlour set aside for VADs and headed upstairs. The last part of the day came through the window lighting a side of the crucifix above the dormitory door. "Poppa and Johnny wouldn't approve of that," she mused, as she took clean clothes, soap and towel to the washroom, where the nuns had mercifully installed a bidet.

After the briefest of prayers beside her cot, she snuggled

under the army issue blankets, and with Noah Oldfield and John Alex still in her thoughts, she inquired of the dark how she could bring them into an awareness of the new woman – women like Helen and herself and all the wartime women workers who were doing what otherwise was thought of as men's work. But, before any plan could form in her head, she was asleep.

★   ★   ★

At the end of March, the Battle of Verdun had reduced that old city to rubble. In England, an anxious curiosity prevailed. When would the allies put in a counter offensive?

Helen Church used all her spare time gathering material for her articles. She had mailed one to the Halifax Morning Herald about young women in a TNT factory, their faces turned yellow by the fumes. She was gathering material for a second article, while watching a seventeen-year-old operate the 'monkey' machine that compressed explosive into shell cases, when a shell exploded, killing Helen, the girl and two other young women.

At St. Luke's, the matron called Jessica into her office. "Miss Church is dead. We just received word a few minutes ago. She was your friend, and we want you to be one of the first to know. Explosion at Brixton Shell Works."

There was a silence in which the room seemed to spin and the blood drained from Jessica's head. "Miss Curtis," barked the matron, "Help me put this girl on the sofa. Miss Merton, get a blanket. Get some smelling salts. Hurry up!"

Some days later, as Jessica returned from a walk, the matron met her in the vestibule with a letter. "We found this in the effects of Miss Church. It's addressed to you."

She ran up the two flights of stairs to the dormitory, and sitting on the edge of her cot, opened the sealed letter and began to read:

Dearest Jessica,

For some time, I've had the strangest premonition — maybe not strange at all, under the circumstances — that I will not live to the end of the war or see home again. If I should suddenly be called by God — and 'suddenly' is the appropriate adverb if we look around — I want to let you know of my great happiness in our friendship.

Although you are an Upper Canadian and I am a Maritimer, we have discovered that we are true sisters. Among the few people I have met over here, you alone have appreciated what I want to achieve and supported me when others gave no encouragement.

The war, with all its evil, is also the dawn of a new age. The tutelage in which ordinary women have been held for millennia is coming to an end. Let us hope that war itself, and all the political machinations that bring on war, will also end when this madness ends.

The fact that the contribution of hundreds of thousands of women here and in the dominions is both sustaining the war effort and providing for the daily needs of millions is telling me that there is now an irreversible tide that will carry women on to full emancipation.

Dearest Jessica, let us be fully committed as women to our God-given dignity and the promotion of women's rightful place under the sun.

The other night there was a great rumbling of wheels in the road. You were sleeping like an angel when it wakened me, yet there was no activity outside. I've

*heard tell that the sound of wheels in the night is notice
that a life will be taken.*

*I am not afraid. Remember me. God bless you and
Johnny.*

> *Carry on!*
> *Affectionately,*
> *Helen*

Jessica folded the letter gently and sat in the vast
emptiness of a grief beyond tears. Looking at what was
Helen's cot across the aisle, she spoke out as though to
Helen's ghost. "As God is my helper, I'll try."

The bell sounded for the evening meal. She put the
letter back in its envelope and into her valise, then descended
slowly to the refectory holding onto the railing.

The next few days were difficult, but Jessica bore up,
stiffened by the matron's words at her orientation. "The nurse
or volunteer who cannot keep a curb on her emotions cannot help the wounded." And, she told herself, Helen would
never lie down on the job whatever the circumstances.

With a few hours off, Jessica could easily slip down to
Queen's Hill by motor coach. On a soft spring day, she gave
John Alex a letter as they sat in the garden. "From Poppa," she
said.

He opened it quizzically. "Why it's on company letter-
head," he said.

"What's so odd about that?" she invited.

"Well nothing, I suppose – just a minute, Jess, says he's
making a proposition for me…"

"Read it top to bottom, darling – top to bottom."

He straightened it out and started reading aloud:

Dear Johnny,

I'm making a proposition to you and I want you and Jessica to give it serious consideration.

Since you left, the business has almost overrun me. This won't be a simple little spring and axle foundry anymore. With war contracts, I've had to put on another shift and add machines. After the war, our future with the company is going to be tied to the automotive industry.

I'm now reaching an age when there will be too much for me to handle. I need a partner and Jessica tells me you are taking cost accounting over there by correspondence. That is the kind of background that will be useful along with all your experience and knowledge of our operation gained in your four years with us.

And the other thing is, and there is no use beating around the bush, I want to keep the business in the family.

I want your answer soon and in the affirmative that you will accept partnership in Royal Spring and Axle Company.

Yours truly,

Noah Oldfield

P.S. Miss Henty and Mrs. Oldfield know about this, but otherwise it is confidential until I hear from you.

"Well, I'll be…" said John Alex.

"What do you think?" she asked him.

"Well…"

"I'll tell you what you think, shall I. You think yes. It's a wonderful opportunity for all of us. Just think, Royal Spring and Axle Company, N. Oldfield and J.A. Tyrone, Proprietors.

His mother's words flashed into his mind, "Your father

made his mark... you will have an opportunity." Here was proof of that in Noah Oldfield's letter. The serendipity of it made him smile.

"What's so funny, darling?" Jessica asked.

"Nothing... nothing. Just remembering something my mother said when I was a kid – that I'd get an opportunity to make my mark. Not many fellows are going to be as lucky as this when the war is over."

She gave him one of her beautiful smiles. "Lucky, you say lucky? After all you've been through. Don't think for a moment Poppa is offering you a bed of roses. There'll be lots of hard work and headaches. How could anything be more obvious? He wants what we want."

"Which is?"

"That we get married, dumbbell."

For a long while, they sat in silence. Finally, John Alex said, "They're taking the cast off tomorrow. I'll be starting exercises." Jessica kissed him. "Praise the Lord, Johnny. When you can get about, we'll start planning the nuptials."

"That may take a time. How do you think your parents are going to feel, if we tie the knot over here?"

"They were young once too. We agreed at New Year's, didn't we? They'll understand."

"Agreed for a second time," he said, "Agreed."

★　　★　　★

When she came back the following week, he was hopping about using crutches. The wounded knee was scarred and misshapen. The full length of his leg was still baby pink after its long confinement in the cast. The doctors had saved the knee – after a fashion – but would it ever bend? His efforts at walking, if that's what it could be called, were painful. But, at least, he was free to move about, shed of the wheelchair.

★   ★   ★

The Battle of the Somme was the 'Big Push' John Alex saw coming; a colossal allied effort and a blood bath without precedent. Before the attack on July 1, British and French forces bombarded enemy positions for seven days with more than a million and a half shells. Twenty thousand British troops died the first day in the largest land battle since Waterloo. At the battle's end in November, the allies had gained only a few kilometres of no strategic importance. The Germans lost 650,000, the British 420,000 and the French 195,000.

The Somme push brought an avalanche of misery requiring the deployment of thousands of doctors, nursing sisters, orderlies and volunteer aides – a deployment, that by mid–August, shifted Jessica out of St. Luke's in London into a mud-spattered casualty-clearing station behind the Somme lines. By mid–October, she was bone-weary, traumatised, and unable to continue.

During the first months of the battle, the staggering cost of lives swept over Britain and the dominions in wave after wave of grief. John Alex was nearly paralysed with anxiety – helpless to do anything for the one who meant more to him than life itself.

His spirits lifted in early November, for Jessica was granted leave to recuperate in England. The roles were reversed. It was his turn to visit her, and he had permission from the doctor who had replaced his crutches with a cane.

He would never regain full use of his bad knee. It was rigidly inflexible; incapable of being a functioning knee; reduced to serving only as a link between his upper and lower leg. "At least, it's better than a peg leg," he told Lieutenant Archie McLean, with whom he had earlier discussed the snootiness of the English officers.

It wasn't the crippling injury that had ever depressed him. On that score, he was grateful and amazed to be merely alive. The depression – the darkness he continued to experience – was the result mainly of the absolute horror of his time in Flanders, the loss of the Fenton boys, and the impossibility of shaking his nightmares and flash-backs when the roar, the pounding, the thudding, the screams and the stench returned. The censored press reports from France – the truth of which he scorned – pushed him further into the pit of despair. His imagination latched onto the truncated news and vivified the obfuscations.

Jessica's proximity and safety was to him as a rope to a drowning man. And, the beauty of it was that he could get from Maidstone, near Queen's Hill, to Luton where she was billeted in little more than an hour by train. On his first visit, she met him in the lace-curtained front room. Her appearance visibly shocked him. She had lost twenty pounds. Her khaki jacket hung like a sack on her spare frame. Heavy rouging couldn't conceal the underlying pallor, nor the dark rings about the eyes. "I know what you're thinking," she said after they kissed lightly. "I'll be back in the pink, you'll see. Mrs. Brown is a dear and I'm being looked after royally. You're to stay for tea and you'll see what I mean." They sat after tea holding hands on the chesterfield, nuzzling and kissing until he had to leave to catch the last train connecting to

Maidstone. In the vestibule, they embraced passionately. "I'll be right as rain in no time," she said.

They married on January 18, 1917 – a month shy of his twenty-fifth birthday. She was twenty-four. They honeymooned three days in a small Sussex inn, finding an island of peaceful bliss in a world where civilization had come unstuck in the trenches of France. Peaceful, but not forgetful or unmindful – the peace drawing strength from one another. They both knew what it was to be dangled above the abyss by the slender thread of existence. They spoke of it. They marvelled at it. And, when one or the other fell silent, it was to reflect on the miracle, the grace of God, that had saved them singly and for each other.

★   ★   ★

In February, the doctors at Queen's Hill decided that everything that could be done for John Alex had been done. He was ready for discharge from the hospital and from military service. On March 11, he disembarked from the S.S. Tripoli in Halifax, immediately entrained for Toronto. He wired Amy from Moncton, "Arr. Union 14:00 Mon. J.A." and was met by the Oldfields and MacLarens upon his arrival.

As their son-in-law, there was no question in Stella's mind that John Alex would stay with them. Amy MacLaren didn't contest. She told Dan on the way to the station. "When Mrs. Oldfield's mind is made up – it's made up!"

Arriving at Oldfield's, Noah went ahead to open the unlocked door. John Alex followed, taking the veranda steps one at a time. Stella, holding Jimmy's hand, and then Amy followed, while Dan carried John Alex' Gladstone bag.

Saying little, they sat in the front room. It was a new

reality having John Alex back, but without Jessica. There was an unnatural strangeness in the situation and her absence weighed heavily. They were prepared — Jimmy included — for John Alex' disability. They weren't prepared for the tautness in his handsome face and the remoteness in his eyes.

Stella moved with precision in the kitchen getting supper, as the others fumbled with conversation in the living room. From the day that Jessica's letter arrived with the news that John Alex was returning, Stella had carefully planned for this evening. The meal would consist of what she remembered John Alex fancied — wartime shortages permitting. Moments after Amy called on Saturday to say John Alex was arriving, she struck out with Jimmy to the butchers, where to her delight, she was able to get his last piece of flank steak to make mock duck with sausage stuffing. When she called them to the table, it was Jimmy who captured the moment. "Look Johnny," he said gleefully pointing at the sideboard, "Momma make apple pie for Johnny."

During the meal, both Amy and Stella guardedly studied John Alex. After, while cleaning up in the kitchen, Amy said, "He's different, but no wonder when you think of what he's been through." Stella nodded thoughtfully.

At the same time, Noah in the living room was passing a box of expensive cigars set aside for the occasion. A few minutes later, the Fentons dropped by. After showing their great pleasure in John Alex' return, they found seats and the room lapsed into silence. Presently, John Alex got to his feet, tapped the end of his cigar in an ash tray on the piano, and looking directly at the Fentons, said, "Privilege to be with Stanley and Frank," in a manner that invited no response.

When Amy and Stella joined them, the evening brightened with discussion about Jessica, now back at St. Luke's in London. How did she look? How much longer did he think she'd be over there? What did she wear for the wedding and the honeymoon?

Later, settling down to sleep in the Oldfield's guest room, a peace came over him. His thoughts, at first, were of Jessica and then, half asleep, he thought of an evening when his mother Joanna put him to bed in the little room under the eve and he said his prayers with her, his eyes closed:

Now I lay me down to sleep,
I pray the Lord my soul to keep,
If I should die before I wake,
I pray the Lord my soul to take.

Then he remembered opening his eyes and asking, "Where does the Lord take my soul?"

"Johnny, you're not to think about that," his mother said, "but if God takes your soul, it will be to the same place as all the rest of us – heaven."

Pulling at her sleeve, he'd asked what heaven was like. Did dogs and horses go to heaven?

"Well now," she said, "heaven is a mighty big place, so there are dogs and horses. Mrs. Minty believes that in heaven, God sits on a great white throne, but he probably walks around quite a bit too. Just between you and me Johnny, do you know what I really believe heaven is like? Heaven is like coming home to your family that loves you. You will under-stand that some day."

He remembered her kissing him goodnight and the lingering scent of lavender, as she blew out the lamp and left him in the darkness.

He shifted in bed to ease the bad knee. "Heaven is home," he mused, "coming home, what else?"

★   ★   ★

Two days later at three in the afternoon, John Alex stepped down from Number 10 at Humber Bend. The stationmaster saw him, straight away went up to him and said, "Great balls of fire! It's Tyrone back from the war." A small group formed around him, peering into his face, pumping his hand, and slapping his back.

Before long, he was delivered by buggy to the house by the mill. He went through the gate and around through the summer kitchen and on in until he found his mother sitting near the coal heater crocheting, while old William was stretched out on a sofa by the wall. She dropped her work to the floor and embraced him, with tears in her eyes. "Can it be?" she said, excitement flooding her voice. William came up before him, while he was still hugging Joanna, and smiling widely, placed his gnarled hand on his shoulder. His eyes filled with the glory of John Alex, still in uniform. Then Joanna, giving her son a kiss on the cheek, disengaged herself and went through the summer kitchen to where the rain barrel stood and called out to the drive shed, "Fred, Fred go quickly... get Watt and Ella. John Alex is home from the war. Hurry... Hurry!"

They had a wonderful evening. And, as at Oldfield's the evening before, no one referred to his limp.

The following morning, John Alex and Joanna walked uptown. The cold March sun was just beginning to melt the snow at the side of the road. He raised the collar of his greatcoat to ward off the chill wind gusting from the river. Joanna, wrapped in fur, walked behind for the winter sidewalk couldn't take two abreast.

A farmer, waiting for his Clyde to be shod, spied them approaching the blacksmith's. "Come out, Anvil!" he yelled, "It's John Alex Tyrone come back from the war." The blacksmith pounded the last nail into the Clyde's front hoof and let it drop with a thud. Reeking of horse's hoof, he came out into the sunlight to greet John Alex. "So, it's you, my caber-tossing buck," he grinned, offering his forge-blackened hand, "I hear you gave the Hun as good as you got. We're all proud to know you, John Alex. And you won a medal and all – you, who wouldn't even raise your dukes to defend yourself. Beats all, I'd say."

Joanna said, "Yes Angus, it's wonderful that our Johnny is home alive and…" She caught herself in time, and then repeated, "…home alive." As they went along Main Street – now abreast for the sidewalk was wider – the stores emptied to greet their returning hero. They all took in his cane and stiffened gait, feigning not to notice as they came up to him. Although, the aging milliner, Hattie Longford, couldn't suppress her tears as she rushed back into the shop, hand over mouth. At last, they fetched up at Strabane's Hardware. Still vigorous after all these years, Donald Strabane greeted his daughter and grandson with a face full of pleasure and a smile that exposed the gold caps of his upper bicuspids. After the first flurry of greetings, Alexander said, "Be a good man Billy and put on a pot of tea. Get the can of cookies out of my desk."

It tickled John Alex to be with his grandfather again and in the store he remembered so well. It had hardly changed from his boyhood, with the same pungent odour of the oiled floor mixed with the redolence of turpentine, rope and nails, and the same chocka block plenitude of things for farm and household. This too was home. This was peace. This was the way the world was meant to be – harmonious, pleasing to the senses, and the antithesis of Ypres, Mouse Trap Farm and St. Julien.

Colin Wilson, village reeve, joined the little celebration. Since his son Todd went off to war, Wilson was short-handed at the creamery, always pressed for time to properly manage his business and take care of the reeve's responsibilities. Having cooled his tea by saucering and blowing on it, he faced John Alex and said, "Council wants you to come tonight for our sitting at seven... I trust you got my message on this Mrs. Tyrone... We normally meet on alternate Tuesdays, but understand you have to get back to the city tomorrow, John Alex. Have a little presentation we want to make."

John Alex, somewhat taken aback, opened his mouth to demur, but noticed his mother behind the reeve's shoulder with her forefinger over her lip. "Sure, glad to," he said. The reeve said, "Well then, see you tonight," tipped his hat to Joanna and left without further comment.

After a supper that required extra boards for the dining room table, Mrs. Minty was left to do the clean-up, while the extended Tyrone-Strabane family trooped down Maple Street to the village hall and up the back steps to the council chamber where they took seats usually occupied by citizens waiting to complain about assessments or to apply for property easements. Seated at the council table, the reeve was flanked by Nelson Broad, the post master and clerk of council, E.G. Toplady, the owner of the Queen's Hotel, the current village doctor, George Short, and a mannish retired farmer Thea Guardhouse.

The reeve stood and said, "On behalf of council and the citizens of Humber Bend, I welcome to this special meeting of council, Captain John Alexander Tyrone, M.C. and his family. We will start as usual, with the national anthem. Please stand and face the flag. That ritual observed, they all sat again, their chairs making a loud clattering on the plank floor. The reeve cleared his throat and, in the ensuing silence, read from a text prepared just that day in the creamery. "Friends, a good number of our young men and even two of our young women have responded to the call of King and Country, none more bravely or gallantly than Captain Tyrone. Over these past months, we have given a lot of time and thought to a suitable expression of gratitude for the patriotism and sacrifice of our native sons and daughters in the war. In due course, Captain Tyrone, we will be erecting a cenotaph to commemorate the names of the men like you, some who, like yourself, will return and some who will never return.

"In anticipation of your return, this council, on behalf of the citizens of Humber Bend, has directed me to get a suitable gift as a mark of our proud esteem for you. Mr. Joseph McCaul, your old teacher agreed to do this for us some time ago and it is regretted he cannot be here at this time." During the reeve's remarks, reported in the Humber Bend Advertiser as "a few well-chosen words," there were sounds of agreement throughout the chamber, with husky voices saying "here, here" and much rapping of canes on the floor, then the reeve handed John Alex a green paperboard box containing the collected poems of Bliss Carman in two vellum-covered volumes. The flyleaf of each volume had been inscribed by McCaul in his flawless script, save for the date, put in carefully on March 14 by the reeve:

Presented to Captain John Alexander Tyrone, M.C.
in recognition of his brave service to King and Country
NON SIBI SED PATRIAE
The Village of Humber Bend
14 March 1917

★ ★ ★

Joseph McCaul never married. He and his single sister Mary Ann lived on what had come to be known as McCaul's Lane on the edge of the village. There was a crab apple tree in the front of the house and a larger chestnut tree across the road beside a zig-zag cedar rail fence enclosing a small pasture. In May, the blossoming of these trees gave pure joy, but this was a drafty March morning following the presentation to John Alex. The trees were leafless and joyless, as he pulled the doorbell at McCaul's.

Mary Ann McCaul came immediately, her thin face full of pleasure as she opened the door. "We hoped you'd come, John Alex," she said, taking his coat and hat. "Joseph is upstairs in his room – it's too much for him to come down. He sleeps, but he doesn't eat much. Dr. Short says there is nothing for it. My, it's good to see you."

The narrow enclosed staircase without railings gave John Alex some difficulty, but he clumped up them and into the room where McCaul was propped up in bed. The blind had been raised and there was a slight whiff of urine.

John Alex had never seen McCaul, other than in good health and dressed carefully in a suit and tie. Even though the man was sick in bed, John Alex was not prepared to find his old teacher so pale and gaunt. It was McCaul who spoke first. "It's alright, Tyrone. Comes to everyone – the end, I mean. Good to see you. Thanks for coming. Very considerate. Don't suppose they told you I only have a short time left... Going to be very hard on Mary Ann. Sit down. I'm delighted to see you. What can you tell me about modern warfare?" John Alex pulled the only chair up and sat parallel to the bed with his bad leg facing the window. "It's hell, sir, pure hell. That's all that can be said."

"Yes, yes," agreed McCaul, trying, but failing, to speak with his old fire. "A noisier, dirtier, deadlier game than it ever has been. Heard so. The Trojan War raised to the power of n, so to speak. Tell me, is there a Trojan horse for the allies? – A tie breaker?

"Well, both sides, sir, are over the lines in aeroplanes now. The British have an armoured machine called a tank with men inside it – that's a kind of Trojan horse, except it's not a secret. Could be very helpful, but I don't believe there will be any surprises sprung on the Hun. It'll come down to numbers and fire power.

"And you, Tyrone, it is well with your soul?"

"I think you know, sir, the wounds of war are in the mind, as well as in the body. I've always looked back to Humber Bend and people like you, sir, to get me through."

"Hmmm, and they say you're married now. How is your wife, overseas still isn't she?"

John Alex took a moment, smiled, and replied, "Yes, she is still in England. Served at the Somme assisting the wounded."

"That's noble," McCaul's voice was weak, barely a hoarse whisper. "Noble indeed. Are you familiar with those lines at the end of Proverbs, 'A good wife who can find? She is far more precious than jewels'."

McCaul was drained. After some time, John Alex said, "I've a train to meet, sir," and awkwardly got to his feet trying not to shake the bed. McCaul looked affectionately at him, a slight glint returning to his eyes. "Thanks again for coming Tyrone. Say hello to your people. God bless you."

★　★　★

On graduating from the University of Toronto, Nathan Fine went into his father Jacob's business, sharing the same cluttered office. On the shop floor, his conversation with the foreman was a terse dialogue of shouts above the whirr of sewing machines. Some of the women workers he knew well enough to greet by name in the street. One in particular was Rose Syrkin, for his father and her father had emigrated together from Russia, but their paths never crossed socially.

At the time, she was just a face among the other faces in the dusty light of the shop. Until, that is, one noon hour when the machines were stilled for lunch. He was on his way across the shop floor to the washroom when he passed Rose, stopped dead, looked around to be certain of what he had just seen, and broke into an uncontrollable fit of laughter. "What's funny?" she asked, "You never see a chestnut being cracked?"

He took a moment to get himself under control. "Sure, seen lots of chestnuts being cracked, but that's the first I've seen cracked with the heel of a shoe." She flushed and looking straight at him said, "Now you have," and though she had other nuts to crack, bent over and put the shoe back on her foot with a swift deftness. Standing with one hand on the uncracked chestnuts, the other clenching her slim hip, she gave him a radiant smile and said, "Okay?"

It was his turn to flush. "Okay, sure I never said it wasn't okay." Something like an electrical shock pulsed through him and from that moment, Nathan Fine knew he loved Rose Syrkin. Soon after, it became obvious to everyone at the Jacob Fine Suit Company (the boss, the accountant, the foreman, the forelady, the cutters, the sewers, the pressers, the basters, pullers, fillers and button-hole makers) that Nathan Fine and Rose Syrkin were in love.

When Nathan approached Jacob about marrying Rose, Jacob just grunted and said, "Will speak with Mendele," her father. He had been waiting for this – hoping for it. Unknown to Nathan, he had been keeping an alert eye for a suitable bride from the day of Nathan's bar mitzvah. Rose Syrkin, as it happens, was first on the list, which included Golda Levine, his accountant's red-haired daughter, and Marie Ganz, the Kensington fishmonger's daughter. "She is a rose," he told Adah, his wife in Yiddish, "a rose of Sharon, a lily among thorns."

Nathan had already started to methodically and passionately court Rose with walks in Trinity Park, boxed chocolates, picnics on Hanlan's Point and other venues free of 'Gentiles Only' signs. Her brother Max tagged dutifully along, always careful to keep a discrete distance. Watching the threesome off on a spring evening, Ruth Syrkin turned to her husband Mendele and said, "There is no such thing as a man having a bad name for giving way to temptation – a woman, that's different."

As the courtship progressed, Rose was soon caught up in Nathan's determination to better the lot of workers. Unlike John Alex Tyrone, whose polestar was an idealized British Empire, Nathan's inspiration came from the promise of socialism. As far as he was concerned, the war had no discernible rationale in morality or necessity. His closest friends held the same anti-war convictions. Conscription put some of them in uniform, but he was rejected because of his chronic asthma.

The consequence of being a non-uniformed young male, and a Jew, had its painful moments. Travelling by streetcar, he would frequently draw hostile glances and was sure other riders were muttering calumny about him.

One nasty experience galled him for months. On a humid June morning, he was waiting outside a buyer's office, when he overheard through the open transom what was being said behind the closed door.

"Mr. Fine is outside, Mr. Stone."

"Alright, someone should boot that young kike down to the enlistment office. Show him in."

The embarrassed secretary opened the door and said, "Mr. Stone will see you now, Mr. Fine."

"Come in," said Stone, leaning back in his swivel chair. "How are things with our good friends in the House of Fine?"

Smarting but controlled, Nathan replied, "The House of Fine is prospering, thanks to customers like yourself giving us orders they can't get filled elsewhere."

"Sure, sure," the buyer retorted, smile gone from his face. "Can you fill this order?" he asked, flicking a typed sheet across the desk to Nathan.

★   ★   ★

Rose Syrkin's parents, Mendele and Ruth, emigrated from Russia to Canada in the 1890s, from the same shtetl as Jacob and Adah Fine. Like the Fines and thousands of other East European Jews, they were 'Luftmenschen' – *people made of air* – victims of the Jewish pogroms of Czar Alexander III and Czar Nicholas II. They arrived in Toronto with the clothing on their backs, a few family valuables stitched into their coats, and the *sine qua non* for survival under the czars – a trade.

A diamond cutter, Mendele soon found employment with Standard jewellers on Queen Street. Jacob exchanged the few gold rubles hidden in his overcoat for enough Canadian dollars to start a tailoring business in the front of their flat in Kensington Avenue.

In 1902, he was doing business in three rooms above the Workers' Academy on Spadina Avenue. He remained there until the outbreak of war in 1914, when his business rapidly expanded to keep up with the demand for army uniforms. In January 1915, he rented the full second floor above Canadian-American Importers and Exporters, just down the street from the Workers' Academy. By 1917, the Jacob Fine Suit Company employed forty-two men and sixteen women with a weekly payroll of nearly fifteen hundred dollars.

For some time, Nathan had been quietly pulling back from Jewish observances. In this, he was encouraged by his Uncle Joseph, self-employed in a little blacksmith shop in the lane behind Augusta Avenue. Joseph was pulled towards socialism in the shtetl where he and Jacob were raised, a pull that was strengthened in the Lower East Side of New York before he moved to Toronto. Many a Sabbath afternoon, uncle and nephew strolled the neighbourhood streets, arm in arm, exchanging views. For them, religion was synonymous with superstition. They could live without it. But, both of them wanted to avoid any open rift with family and friends, or be seen denying the Jewish identity. They were free thinkers. They were socialists. They would never be gentiles.

In Nathan's mind, it was only sensible, no matter how forthright or outspoken Uncle Joseph could be at times on religion and politics, that he himself soften the edges of his convictions when talking with his parents. Instinctively, he knew that their mutual love could bridge whatever gulf separated them, and he was anxious that nothing weaken that bridge. Thus, when the marriage was approved by both the Fine and Syrkin elders, he agreed, as did Rose, to have the wedding in the synagogue where Jacob and Mendele had been two of the founders. Not only that, but he would also allow his father to request that their cousin, Rabbi Samuel Fine of Buffalo, come and officiate. All the proprieties were met and a date set for May 11, 1917 – the Rosh Hodesh of Sivan.

The Syrkins hadn't means to give Rose the traditional dowry they would have preferred. No matter, there was crystal and linen purchased with great care in the better stores on Yonge Street. Nathan, with a generous loan from Uncle Joseph, bought the finest gold ring he could find, which on the happy nuptial day, he placed on the bride's index finger repeating after Rabbi Fine, word for word in Hebrew, "Be you consecrated unto me by this ring, in accordance with the laws of Moses and Israel."

*   *   *

Like Royal Spring and Axle, the Jacob Fine Suit

Company prospered through the war years. By the time of Nathan's marriage to Rose, Jacob was able to move the family north in the city to a neighbourhood of substantial homes set behind trim front lawns.

On the day they drove up with the agent to see the house, Adah whispered in the ear of her youngest, "David, is just like country."

After a brief honeymoon in Niagara Falls, Nathan and Rose moved into the third floor of the new house and shared meals with the family, including the traditional Sabbath meal when Adah served her steaming chicken soup, and lighting three candles pronounced the blessing that brought in the day of rest, "Barukh attah, vetzivanu lehadik, ner shel Shabbat."

As likely as not, Rose and Nathan would not be present for the end of the Sabbath "when three stars appear in the sky" and a prayer is said in anticipation of Messiah's coming. They would, instead, be downtown at a labour meeting or at one or another socialist conclave. "It's superstition to believe that God will give us the future out of the blue – just by waiting," Nathan told Rose.

Their gradual detachment from the rites and customs of Jewish faith naturally disturbed Jacob and Adah, who nevertheless kept their peace. Both couples felt the strain occasioned by their different approach to the Sabbath, dietary restrictions, and holy days.

Putting her good wares away after a Sabbath, Adah mused that the harmony in the family is like fine crystal – beautiful, but also fragile if care is not taken. With the emotional temperature cooling month by month, she became increasingly apprehensive that young David would become infected by his older brother's agnosticism – something she

116

put down to the baleful influence of her brother-in-law Joseph.

She was searching for something to say – perhaps it could be from the Torah – something indirect that could be dropped into the supper conversation, oh so gently, like a leaf on the door sill of consciousness. But, before she could fully weigh the place and usefulness of interjecting the injunction from the Torah that in marriage "a man leaves his father and mother and cleaves to his wife", her immediate concern was put to rest by Nathan's announcement that he and Rose had found an apartment downtown on College Street. "It's above a bakery and the smell is wonderful, Momma," he told her, while Jacob stood by noncommittally stroking his beard.

When Nathan and Rose went out that evening, the elder Fines agreed that their decision to move out was a normal thing for a young couple. They would be closer to the Syrkins, and wasn't that natural?

And when Nathan resigned from the suit company to work for the union, Jacob looked steadily at him. "I hope you know what you're doing... my door is always open to you – but I should want a union?" Rose stayed on as a sewer for a time, but when her waist thickened, she too left the business.

– 1919 –

Jessica arrived in Toronto in mid–March, 1919. At the station, John Alex whisked her off her feet, almost losing his balance, and planted a warm kiss on her lips. "Hey, your moustache still tickles," she laughed.

At the Oldfield's, there were fewer people than there might have been before the Spanish flu ran amok. Miss Henty, from the office at Royal Spring and Axle, was one of the victims. The rest of Oldfield's workforce was reduced by a third with sickness. The firm was months behind in filling orders for major customers – all of this worsened by the suppliers, who, for the same reason, couldn't meet their delivery schedules.

Despite the risk of infection, some good friends, neighbours and old classmates came over to the Oldfield's to celebrate Jessica's return. Still in VAD uniform, she had filled out again in recent months and moved easily about chatting and laughing with the guests. At eight o'clock, Stella, Joan Fenton and Robina laid out a grand buffet – an old-fashioned spread with joints of ham and beef, turkey, pumpkin soup, oysters, cheeses and jellied salads, cakes and pies, tea and coffee – but no wine, for Stella forbade alcohol consumption in her house.

The homecoming was covered by West Toronto's *Leader and Recorder* – and the Anglican rector and his wife were there. "I couldn't miss this, if my life depended on it," the rector said when Jessica thanked him for coming. Given the fact that people were wearing masks most of the time in public, this might just have been prophetic.

In bed at last, close to mid-night, Jessica was too tired for what otherwise would have been a normal follow-through to such a reunion.

"Do you know what heaven is?" asked John Alex.

"Heaven is coming home," she said, falling asleep immediately.

★   ★   ★

Some months after the murder of her husband, Charlotte Gunn suggested to Ned that he sell the Moore Park house and move back with Robina to Craigellachie. Her suggestion was prompted, in part, by a desire to keep an eye on Ned, and partly because she was "tired of bumping around by myself in this big place."

So far as Ned and Robina were concerned, there wasn't any reason to refuse Charlotte's invitation. In fact, they liked the idea very much, not least because it could enhance their social position. Charlotte and Robina found it possible to co-exist under the same roof, and the space of Craigellachie appealed to them.

It was a few weeks after returning to West Toronto that Jessica eased her car onto the driveway of Craigellachie. After she and Robina embraced in the portico, the first order of

120

business was to go straight up to the nursery where Robina and Ned's first born was being entertained by her nanny. The birth in the spring of 1918 had been uneventful and the newborn was named Bonnie Ruth. Now a toddler, she went unencouraged to Jessica, who swept her up for a kiss and hug. After some minutes of playing with Bonnie Ruth, they returned her to her nanny and the old friends went downstairs to chat and wait for Charlotte to join them at tea — a ritual that Charlotte was definite about observing precisely at four.

"How's Johnny?" asked Robina, "Does his knee pain him?"

"Not much," replied Jessica, "except on damp days. He does rely on a cane. And Ned, how's he?"

Robina glanced to the door where Charlotte was expected, then turning to face Jessica, she said in a low voice, "Ned's not a well man."

"I had no idea Binny. Has he been sick?"

"Not exactly."

"What then?"

"Drink. Some days he has to be brought home early from the office and some days he's so hung over that he doesn't go to the office. We've had to send for Uncle Jack twice to come and straighten things out. The firm isn't getting new business. Staff are fed up. Nothing and no one seems able to snap him out of it — not his mother, not his old chums, no one."

"I had no idea, Binny," said Jessica, "No idea, at all. You didn't mention anything of the sort in your letters."

"You had enough to contend with, Jess. I didn't want to burden you."

"Yes, and you Fentons are always cheerful. Never complain. See the bright side of everything."

"Not always. There's a lot of uncertainty hanging over us right now. This flu epidemic has forced Ned to close the office on a number of days. One of my best friends down there, Nancy Dalrymple, died last week.

At this point, both women were struggling to control their grief.

"And, that is only the half of it," quavered Robina. "Ned has found a friend, a horrible man, who is filling Ned's head with all kinds of bigoted claptrap about Jews and Italians. Pure drivel. And Neddy is drinking it in. He writes for a rag I won't even allow inside the door *Hold Fast: A Clarion Call for Racial Purity*. It's full of trash about immigrants. I've been told that Neddy and Richard – Richard Bedford is his name, but he writes under the name Theodore Trufax in *Hold Fast* – have been seen downtown together a number of times and mostly under the weather. Someone saw Bedford drunk as a lord on Queen Street push an old peddler and yell at him, 'Go back to Jerusalem!' I'm so ashamed, Jess. Even the polite bigots in Rosedale are beginning to snub us. Neddy has become an embarrassment all round."

. Just then, Charlotte entered the room. "What's going on here?" she asked. "You two look like you just heard about the Titanic. So very good to see you, Jessica. It's been a while. We need to hear about your adventures, but first some tea."

Heading home into the late winter sunset, Jessica could hardly keep her mind on the wheel. So many young Canadians, their lives never lived out, left dead in Europe, and Ned Gunn with a wife and child – privileged Ned Gunn – squandering his life. With fools like Richard Bedford promulgating their cretin opinions, where was the civilization that the war was supposed to save? She felt heavy – very heavy.

Reaching home, Jessica dashed upstairs to sit in the dark, until finally John Alex came up to announce that supper was ready. At bedtime, he refused to turn out the light until she told him everything. Her deep concern stabbed him. He had never had a drinking problem, but he had been guilty of making some thoughtless cracks about immigrants and of laughing at jokes that were nothing more than racial slurs. For the first time, a penetrating light fell on this part of his personality, and he was deeply ashamed.

★   ★   ★

From the living room, they heard the baby's soft cry. "Sounds healthy," said Noah. "So, it's to be Roderick James."

"Sounds very healthy," added Amy. "Why are they calling him Roderick? James I understand. It's a Tyrone name. Why Roderick?"

"Why Roderick? My father's name," clipped Stella. "Jimmy, you already have a piece of cake. Put that back on the tea-wagon."

"It's a miracle we have a baby," offered Noah. "Jimmy, do as Momma says, put that cake back."

"That's a fact," said Amy. "When you consider they came through the war... When you consider that none of us has the flu... touch wood... yes, I'd say a miracle. Definitely a miracle." In the fading day, silence filled the room. By and by, Jimmy got up and switched on the light.

– 1920 –

Amy's comment was premature. In late February, with snow still piled outside, Jessica developed the symptoms. When the doctor came downstairs from her bedside, Stella asked, "What about the baby?"

"Has to be kept away from her. You'll have to find a wet nurse immediately or put him on a bottle. A bottle right away, though. She can't go near him, and keep your fingers crossed that he hasn't got it already." Noah came in the back way. "How is she?" he asked, flinging aside his galoshes.

"She's terrible. Raging fever. Doctor Mavety just left. We have to find a wet nurse, meantime I'm fixing a bottle."

"A wet nurse?"

"That's what I said. Didn't you tell me that Mrs. Grogan just had a baby?"

"You're right, Johnny could ask her to help."

When John Alex put the question to Olga, she said, "For you, Johnny, anything." She had vast bosoms and an overflow of milk. Twice a day, John Alex fetched her to suckle Roderick. More milk was expressed for bottle feedings.

Stella had, for the first time, assumed the responsibility of surrogate mother – not trusting John Alex to do 'women's work'. He wasn't unhappy to be relieved of diaper changing or forgoing sleep at three in the morning.

★   ★   ★

Two weeks later, Dr. Mavety said to Stella, "That's a strong daughter you have, Mrs. Oldfield. She can get up and move about, but keep her clear of the baby for now."

Jessica came downstairs to watch the feedings, grateful for Olga's help – envious as well, for her own supply was dried up.

After the London infirmary, after the hell of the Somme, she had – despite the flu – a great zest for life and the everyday environment around her of familiar street scenes and sounds – the helmeted policeman rolling past on his bicycle, the horse drawn delivery wagons, the small bands of roaming dogs...

A few afternoons later, Olga had left with John Alex, and Stella was watching Roderick in his bassinet. School children were hurrying along in the cold afternoon when Jessica caught sight of a rag and bone man, wagon piled high with old mattresses and springs. "Rags and bones – ra-ags and bo-ones," his call was like a fog horn.

Often the butt of schoolboy taunts, today they added injury to insult when one of their snowballs hit his spavined nag on the muzzle. The animal reared up, then gave a lurch forward, just enough to tip his owner off the seat over the wheels and down into the street where he lay stunned, blood trickling from his temple.

"Momma, momma," Jessica called, "the rag and bone man just fell from his wagon. I think he's hurt. Please – quickly. Roddy will be alright. (Without forethought, she'd used the diminutive 'Roddy' for the first time.)

It only took Stella seconds to reach the man's side. She asked, "Can you move?" He said, "Can't move."

A passing teamster joined her. "I saw what happened," he said. "Those young punks should be thrashed. Won't do for us to lift him."

"Right," said Stella. "I'll get a blanket."

At the living room door, Jessica said, "I'll phone the fire station. They'll send a stretcher."

The fireman arrived quickly and gently got the man into the house and onto the living room sofa. One of them said, "I'm afraid some of the blood is getting onto the sofa."

"Never mind that," snapped Stella. "Thanks for your help."

"We're going to help you," Jessica told him. "What is your name?"

"Name is Kutsher – Augusta Avenue, like it says on wagon."

"Good," said Jessica. "I know that street," and to Stella, "We'll call Nathan, he'll know what to do."

"Nathan?"

"Yes, Nathan Fine – the only Nathan Fine in the phone book."

"I know this Fine you speak," groaned the man.

Roddy had fallen back to sleep. Stella removed him in his bassinet to the dining room table, closing the French doors. He slept quietly on, undisturbed by the sounds and movement in the adjacent room.

A seeming eternity later, Nathan arrived with Uncle Joseph in his father's McLaughlin-Buick. Joseph took charge of the horse and wagon, and with a 'git-up' and a flick of the whip, moved off slowly towards Keele Street.

When Stella brought Nathan into the front room Jessica, who was standing by the fireplace, didn't go over to him but said, "Thanks for responding to our SOS, Nathan."

Looking over to the sofa where Chone Kutsher was stretched, Nathan muttered, "So the old boy is another victim of sheeny baiting." Moving beside the victim, he said clearly "Shalom aleichem, old friend, an ambulance is coming for you."

Kutsher reached out, grimacing, to take Nathan's hand, "Horse and wagon?" he asked.

"Uncle Joseph is taking the wagon back to your stable."

"Is this doctor vaytik room?"

"No, no. You had an accident on the street. These kind ladies are friends of mine. They brought you in here. This is their house."

"Goyim? Gevalt! I should die!"

"Nein, nein, old man, this is not di alte heyn. This is a mitzvah for you by good people."

"Yah, yah," he replied in a whisper.

★   ★   ★

As the ambulance moved from the curb with Kutsher, Nathan said, "Rose's cousin Max is interning at the Western. He'll keep an eye out for him."

"So you know Mr. Kutsher," Jessica said.

"Yes, going back a long time. He gets his horse shod by Uncle Joseph."

"Your uncle who fixed daddy's leaking gas tank?"

"The same."

"I'll make fresh tea," Stella said.

When she left the room, Nathan said to Jessica who was still in kimono and slippers, "You've been ill by the looks of it. The flu?"

"Just getting over it. Trying hard to get on my feet."

"How are Johnny and the baby?"

"Johnny's fine. I've had to get a wet nurse for Roddy. He's behind you through the doors on the dining room table."

Nathan went and looked intently into the bassinet for a good minute. Returning to the living room, he said "Mighty fine. Mighty fine. Can't make out which of you he looks like."

Jessica said, "Nor can we. How's Rose?"

"Rose is so-so. Guess you could say she's depressed. We lost our baby, Sally." His eyes filled and he turned away.

When Stella wheeled in the tea wagon, she found Jessica in the armchair and Nathan at the end of the sofa recently occupied by Chone Kutsher.

"Something wrong?" she asked.

"Momma, it's terrible," said Jessica. Nathan and Rose lost their baby two weeks ago."

"I am sorry, truly sorry, Nathan," she said, and it was the first time she had used his name in speaking to him. Turning to the tea things, she added in a soft voice, "You can't have anything worse than the loss of a child."

★   ★   ★

Days and nights in the mud of Flanders; days and nights convalescing with a shattered knee. Those days and nights wrought a change in John Alex. Gone the cheerful confidence of youth; gone too the unquestioning patriotism of

129

1914. Back in Toronto, he was ready to concede that those who had stayed home on grounds of conscience had a case. Maybe.

He and Jessica remained shaken and sobered by the hellish nightmare of their war experience. There would be no snap of a hypnotist's fingers to bring them back to a pre-war life of innocence or to a sunny forgetfulness. Still, he had work and prospects. They had each other. There were moments of joy, a life to live for — a future.

The day of Chone Kutsher's fall, he came in by the back door at dusk. Jessica greeted him in the kitchen, "Johnny, guess who was here today?"

"A lot of people — bread man, ice man, who?"

"Nathan Fine."

"Nathan Fine. What's he doing these days? Still waging war on employers?"

"Momma went out to help a ragman. Fell from his wagon. Momma called Nathan and he came with his uncle. Took the ragman away by ambulance. Nathan and Rose lost their baby two weeks ago."

John Alex looked at his wife, looked into her eyes, paused and said, "I'm sorry," in a quiet voice.

Jessica said, "I think I'd like to go down and see Rose. Just imagine if we lost Roddy."

"You're calling him Roddy now. Sounds better to me too. But look, hold on now, you have to be a lot stronger than you are now before you do that."

"Yes, boss," she said.

★   ★   ★

April's dull bluster made way for a dazzling Easter

130

Sunday. Shed of their winter coats, the Tyrones came out after dinner to stroll with Roddy in his new carriage.

In the previous weeks, housebound with the flu and its enervating aftermath, Jessica had been quietly ruminating about the direction of her life as well as their need to get a home of their own. Half seriously and half as a lark, she had confronted Stella one morning as they washed breakfast dishes.

"If something happened to Poppa, do you think you could run Royal Spring in his place?"

"What prompts that?" Stella retorted. "Johnny would step in."

"But let's say, for argument's sake, that Johnny wasn't in the picture. Could you fill Poppa's shoes?"

"Well, I'd need some help in the beginning, but yes, I could take over if it came to that. How the customers and the men on the floor would take it – that's a completely other matter. This is fanciful talk, isn't it?"

"Yes and no. Yes and no. I'm of a mind that women can do far more than they're given credit for. It's a matter of opportunity and a matter of how somewhere in the past the division of labour was handed out"

"You get that from Nathan?"

"Nathan and others."

★   ★   ★

Out on the sidewalk, John Alex attention focused on keeping his handicapped gait in rhythm with Jessica's as she pushed Roddy along.

"Johnny do you know what the war did?"

"Drive up the price of oats. Topple the Kaiser. What?"

"It changed the situation of women, that's what."

"The federal vote? That's good. Even your father thinks so."

Yes, and by George, we are soon going to have the provincial vote. But you're missing my point."

They stopped to show off Roddy to the Fentons heading in the opposite direction. "Be a darling and put Roddy's rattle back in his hand," said Jessica. "Is his bonnet on too tight? No? I guess it's okay. Getting back to the subject, as I said, you're missing the point."

"Nothing new there," quipped John Alex, slowing down to light a cigarette, cane crooked over his elbow. "What am I missing?"

"Remember Helen Church?"

"Yep."

"It was she who said that the war would change everything for women. Dawn of a new age, full emancipation. Do you know Johnny, I've kept her one and only letter to me along with yours and I look at it a lot – think about it a lot. And she was right."

"I'm listening."

"The point I'm making is quite simple and it affects us – you and me. The point is that during the War, the powers that be, for the first time in history, discovered that women can do just about anything men can do, and a few things men can't do."

"And don't want to do," added John Alex.

"Face it, Johnny. British and French women are our example, but not just them."

"The Bolsheviks?"

"Drop the sarcasm. I'm serious. What would allies have

done without the farmerettes... the munitionettes... the boat-yard workers – and all for less than men's wages."

"So Jessica, what are you driving at? Fifty-fifty in the labour force. Women replacing men throughout industry, even government and the church eventually. Don't you see, it can't add up."

"Oh, it adds up alright. And not just in the run of the mill manual jobs. Women can also hold their own intellectually. Four years at university proved that to me. There are going to be more female Nobel Prize winners like Marie Curie. And more and more." Her voice had become a little shrill, then as abruptly as the conversation had started, it ended. She smiled at him and said, "Sorry darling. It just had to come out. It's a little heavy for an Easter outing."

It still didn't add up to John Alex. But still, again, she was nobody's fool...

- 1936 -

The Gunn's were at rock bottom. Just days before Ned's death in the General Hospital from cirrhosis of the liver, Robina and her two daughters, Bonnie Ruth and Maxine, moved into a small apartment on Wellesley Street. Sir John Clarke, recently separated from his cantankerous wife, stood the costs.

Despite the pinch of the Depression, Robina was able to find work in the Circulation Department of the Evening Telegram, Toronto's other afternoon and evening newspaper. At a company dance, she met Russell Dawe from the City Desk. They married and settled into a house in the Beach with the two girls.

Robina and Jessica remained close. For a few summers in the Thirties the Dawes vacationed in the Tyrone's guest house at their summer residence – Royal Summer – on Lake of Bays.

Roddy and the Gunn girls spent hours sunning on the dock, boating and playing tennis – even pitching horseshoes.

In the summer of 1936, Jessica's housemaid said to her, "I think Roddy has a crush on Maxine." It did look that way. They were increasingly off by themselves, separated from

Bonnie Ruth who had started to read serious English and American authors, spurred on by Russell Dawe.

Maxine and Roddy were inseparable – driving into Huntsville for ice cream sundaes; playing rummy into the late evening.

The culmination of all this propinquity came in the guest house one Sunday evening, when the others were in the main building listening to the Jack Benny Show. Roddy and Maxine were stretched out on the grass mat in a passionate embrace when Bonnie Ruth came in without warning to get her cardigan and nearly fell over them.

They scrambled to their feet with sheepish grins. Bonnie Ruth just smiled as Maxine straightened her hair and looked past her.

*　　*　　*

One August morning in the summer of Maxine and Roddy's infatuation, Bonnie Ruth asked if she could look through the Tyrone photograph albums. Normally, these were kept in the city, in the room intended originally to be John Alex's study – a room with walnut panelling and fashionable casement windows. Over the years this had become the repository of family history, a cornucopia of framed photographs covering the desk and climbing the walls.

To the annoyance of John Alex – but nevertheless – a number of albums were toted to Royal Summer annually, in a cloth covered butter box kept from Jessica's school days, and placed beside a front room window overlooking the lake.

That August morning in 1936, they opened an album on the dining room table and Jessica, flanked by the two sisters, went through it for the better part of an hour. The girls were totally absorbed, devouring each picture with great interest and the carefully notated explanation below it in white ink.

The screen door banged behind Roddy on his way to the dock and then a second bang as Jimmy followed him.

Just then Maxine was saying, "It's Mommy with Aunt Jessica on skates." And Bonnie Ruth said, "That's Jimmy with his dog Jack. I remember Jack, don't you, Maxine?"

"Are you and Uncle Johnny in this picture of the Tyrone reunion?" Maxine wanted to know.

"Yes," replied Jessica. "Look, that's us in the back row. And there's Roddy. He was six that year – no seven – there seated on the ground with his cousin Upton of Humber Bend." She let that sink in then pointed out John Alex' parents, noting that he was much older than she, and John Alex' half brother, Walt and his half sister, Amy. "You've met Amy at our place, I'm sure."

Below the sterile façade of a two-storied building, Jessica had written 'St. Christopher House.' "What's that?" Bonnie Ruth asked.

"Rightly, St. Christopher Settlement House," said Jessica. "downtown near the Western Hospital. It's a place where they help immigrants."

"What kind of immigrants?" Maxine wanted to know.

"Jewish and Italian mainly."

"Daddy didn't like Jews or Italians. Why was that?" Bonnie Ruth was thoughtful, eyebrows slightly puckered.

"No good reason I can think of," Jessica said gently.

"Did you take this picture Aunt Jessica? Nathan and Rose Fine strike picketing outside Queen City Apparel, September 1923."

"No, that was in the Daily Star and I got a copy from them. The Queen City Apparel strike was a very important one."

Bonnie Ruth's tone was quizzical. "Do strikes interest you Aunt Jessica? Aren't they bad?"

Strikes are bad, Jessica replied. "You can't say they are good because in a strike people often do and say ugly things. But a strike is often the only way a labour union has of forcing the company to pay decently and provide decent working conditions. My friends, the Fines, were getting workers to join the union."

"Are they still your friends? Do they still work for the union? Daddy hated unions."

The innocent earnestness of the questions made Jessica smile. "Yes, they are still my friends- my very good friends," she said. "And yes, they still work for the union. And as for hating unions, your dad was hardly alone – a lot of people hate unions. But you know what – many more people are living better in this world because of unions."

"How's that Aunt Jessica?"

"Well now where can I start... that's a long story... Maybe it would help if you could see inside some of the factories where the workers are. You should be aware that many of them are young women like the workers in Queen City Apparel – and often as not, they work in dirty, dismal, noisy, firetraps for precious little pay." Roddy interrupted with his call from the dock, "Jimmy and I are waiting."

"Guess we'd better go," said Maxine. "Roddy wants us to go with him over to Dwight. Can we do this again, Aunt Jessica?"

As the girls bounded down the lawn, Jessica heard

Jimmy ask Roddy if he would get him an ice cream cone in Dwight. She continued to look at the strike picture. There were about fifty picketers stretched along the sidewalk in front of Queen City Apparel. Three mounted policemen were positioned along the curb.

The day before the picture was taken, police charged up on the sidewalk with night-sticks, a fact attested to obliquely in the picture's cutline:

Workers truculent but orderly after police forced them yesterday to let non-unionized workers cross their picket line into Queen City Apparel. The strike is in its second month.

Looking at Rose's defiant face, Jessica recalled the day in 1920 she went to the Fine's College Street walk-up. Rose was civil but wary, responding to Jessica's expressed sympathy for the loss of her infant with nothing more than "That's life."

This was their first meeting alone. It wasn't what Jessica expected. After an awkward silence, she inquired, "What did you name the baby?"

"Joseph Hill Fine."

"After *the* Joe Hill?"

"What else. And after Nathan's Uncle Joseph.

"Of course," said Jessica quietly.

Another silence. Jessica remembered them sitting in the front room, streetcars rattling below, and the fragrance of fresh bread from the bakery on the first floor. She was semi-reclined in the only easy chair and Rose was upright on a straight-back chair. An ancient roll-top desk, an unlit gas heater, and a crammed bookshelf over which hung a picture of Leon Trotsky, exhorting Russian troops, completed the furnishings.

Rose spoke. "You and Nathan been friends for a long time?"

"Yes, a long time. Nine years."

"And what was it?"

"What was it?"

"Yes, like you were lovers?"

A brake slammed in Jessica's mind. She paused and then said in an even voice. "No, my lover was and is the man I married."

"A boss?"

"You could say that."

"Then what? What is between you and Nathan?"

"Friendship."

"Your husband, he knows about you and Nathan?"

"Absolutely."

"And he's not jealous?"

"At one time. Not now."

"So you just thought: I'm a friend of Nathan. It follows I'm a friend of Rose. Just like that." Rose spoke in a controlled monotone.

"Guess that's it. Never thought of it otherwise. Would you prefer it otherwise, Rose?"

Rose took her time replying. Finally, she broke into a laugh, slapped her thigh and said, "You're a real schlemiel. I like you," and jumping off her chair she went to Jessica and kissed her on the cheek.

"A schlemiel?" Jessica smiled, a question in her voice.

"Forget it," said Rose. "A goy doesn't need to know." She handed Jessica an unfamiliar newspaper. "Nathan likes the Forward – swears by it. Read and I'll make tea."

Now, sixteen years later, in thinking of that day at the

140

Fine's apartment, Jessica had to laugh at herself. "I *was* a schlemiel," she murmured.

★   ★   ★

The screen door slapped. Jessica loved that sound – a sound of summer she said. John Alex thumped in, trailed by Russell Dawe. "Where's Roddy?" he demanded of Jessica.

"Went to Dwight with Jimmy and the girls," she replied. "Why?"

Tapping his cane impatiently on the floor, he said, "I need the boat to get over to Bigwin for a twelve o'clock appointment. I asked him to be back here by eleven thirty. It's almost twelve."

Russell broke in. "Johnny! Look! At the point!"

They raced toward the dock, Jessica beside John Alex, Russell ahead and Robina coming down off the guest house porch to join them.

"It's MacInnes towing our boat," exclaimed John Alex. "Something's wrong alright."

At first the noon glare made it impossible to identify the dark figures in the Tyrone launch. "There's only three," Jessica shouted.

In less than a minute, Roddy came into focus sitting zombie-like behind the wheel. Bonnie Ruth and Maxine were holding each other in the stern seat, sobbing.

Cutting his motor, MacInnes came towards the dock. Jessica clamped her hand over her mouth as Robina moved quickly to steady John Alex. Jimmy lay dead on his back in the bottom of MacInnes' launch, his blue eyes open and facing upward into the noonday sun.

Other than the lap of the lake on the dock, there wasn't

a sound. MacInnes broke the silence. "Best leave him where he is until the police and coroner come."

"The police and coroner?" John Alex was barely audible.

"Yes, in a situation like this, they'll want a statement before they release the body to an undertaker.

When the policeman and coroner arrived, Jessica was up in her room. Roddy was with her. John Alex and the girls sat glumly on the veranda with Robina. Russell Dawe and MacInnes were at the dock.

They re-assembled at the foot of the lawn while the coroner examined the body and the policeman took statements. His report, filed in Huntsville that afternoon, read:

Friday, 17 August 1936 at approx. 11:55 a.m., a launch, property of J.A. Tyrone of Royal Summer Cottage, Bass Point, Lake of Bays, operated by Roderick Tyrone, age 17, son of owner, hit submerged rock near Bass Point. Three passengers thrown into lake on impact, namely, James Oldfield 36, brother of Mrs. J.A. Tyrone, Bonnie Ruth Gunn 17, and sister Maxine 16, guests of the Tyrones, both rescued by R. Tyrone using lifebouy ring secured to launch. James Oldfield presumed dead by drowning when reached by Duncan MacInnes of Sandy Bay, Lake of Bays, who recovered the body. MacInnes was the only other witness to the accident. Separate report from Dr. L.M. Smythe, coroner confirms testimony of R. Tyrone and Gunn sisters that death of James Oldfield result of accidental drowning.

The Tyrones and Oldfields were devastated. At the funeral service in St. John's Anglican church in West Toronto,

142

Roddy was chalk white. Noah Oldfield, failing badly, had to be helped into the church. Stella, ever stoic, sat with ramrod back, her eyes that had been running for two days covered by her veil.

The rector and long-time family friend, Canon Stone, eulogised briefly, "This Jimmy, this sweet, sweet Jimmy, whose development was arrested by some strange quirk of nature which only God in His infinite wisdom and compassion understands — this sweet, sweet Jimmy, loved by us all, God has called suddenly home. He did not suffer at the end. We will miss his golden smile and his friendly disposition. It is a time of particular pain for the family who always surrounded him with tenderest love and care."

The canon had intended to say more but he suddenly cut his eulogy short as Noah gave a moan that filled the nave.

144

- 1938 -

"This is pure heaven," thought Jessica. "Time to think. Time not to think if you choose." She and John Alex were returning on the Princess Mary from a spring holiday in the south of England where they spent three days in the same Sussex inn of their honeymoon, sleeping in the same room, making love in the same bed. In the intervening twenty-one years, nothing had changed.

They visited Queen's Hill, now a veterans' hospital, then St. Luke's in London, which had reverted into an Anglican hospice for travellers of modest means and, finally, Mrs. Brown's in Luton who, now bent and gray, remembered Jessica and her young captain and once again plied them with tea and scones with clotted cream and jelly.

Jessica was comfortably stretched out in a deckchair on the sunny side of the open upper deck, cardigan draped over her shoulders. Far to the south, the Gaspé cliffs shouldered into the Gulf. The afternoon sun felt like a blessing on her face. She laid her book aside, put her head back, closed her eyes, and basked. Yes, time without pressure, an opportunity to reflect on the past and conjure up the future.

An old aphorism occurred to her, one sometimes repeated in sermons and convocation addresses during university days: 'The unexamined life is not worth living.' And about this advice Nathan Fine had once said, "I get the drift alright, but why do we have to hear it all the time?"

As though a curtain lifted on a stage, she saw Roddy just past his toddling days. Jimmy was pulling him in his little wagon between the houses on Annette Street, and she thought of him a little older when he successively had had measles, mumps and chicken pox. It seemed as though the red quarantine card was never out of the window.

Roddy was in school, wearing breeks with leather knee patches, when they moved into the house on Mohawk Park. She could see his freckled face as in the snapshot she carried in her purse. And about then – yes, it must have been a few days after the move, Roddy would be ten, no eleven, and Johnny was like a thundercloud because he had taken Roddy over to Siding Street to see the works and Roddy on the way home said, "Why do people work in a dirty place like that?"

Roddy's reaction to Royal Spring came as no surprise to her. Her own first visit to the works with Noah had been both fascinating and terrifying: all the banging and thumping, the eerie workers in leather gauntlets and smeared leather aprons pocked by sparks, the hissing, the pungent smoky smell; altogether a scene from hell in her childish imagination that gave her nightmares for months. What was so unusual in Roddy's question? But Johnny wasn't thinking in that way. He was only thinking of the implied threat to his dream of a family enterprise that would grow and reach down the years to the glory of the Tyrone name. "For goodness sake, Johnny," she said at the time, "try to reflect on how you viewed things when you were only eleven."

Yet Roddy could be thoughtless. Johnny had said he was spoiled and she supposed he was. But oh how she loved him. Was there anything wrong in that?

That day last summer, Roddy knew that Johnny needed the launch to go over to Bigwin Inn. Took it out anyway with Binny's girls and Jimmy – across the lake and out of sight.

She sat up with a shudder. Jimmy's lifeless form was stretched on the bottom of the launch. They were milling about on the dock trying to understand.

She lay back again and closed her eyes, letting herself be lulled by the sun's warmth on her face, the sea air, the reassuring hum of the distant engines, the mewling gull above the taffrail.

Somewhere forward the sound of a bell. It brought back the ring of the hall phone in the middle of the night.

"Mrs. Tyrone?" a brusque voice inquired.

"Yes."

"Sergeant O'Byrne here, New York State Police. We have your son, Roderick and two others in custody. Bringing him into Jefferson Avenue Police Court, Niagara Falls, at ten o'clock tomorrow morning. If he is to have bail, someone will have to come and post it".

"God almighty," was all that Johnny had said when she came upstairs.

She remembered how they left home in the dark and reached the court with minutes to spare and Roddy standing before the magistrate, pale, dishevelled, charged with drunk driving and property damage to the Ace Truck Diner, while the two others were released without charges.

As though it was yesterday, she could hear Johnny fuming, she had never seen him angrier. "What's come into that boy? We do our best by him, don't we? The car for his eighteenth birthday and he goes down to Buffalo... gets drunk with his pals... probably a dose of clap to boot. Ends up almost killing someone in the middle of the night."

"Calm yourself, calm yourself," she said, putting her arm over his shoulder.

"Calm yourself – calm yourself," he shouted, "Hell's bells, Jess, I can't believe this is happening to us. Your father built up the company; turned it over to us and we've built it more. A business to be proud of – over a million in assets. A family enterprise. Something for Roddy to build on in his turn. But will he – will he? His behaviour recently suggests something else."

She remembered he took a long time to cool down and her saying, "I think I'm in a better frame of mind than you to talk to him Johnny. He's got a come-uppance and after his court appearance, he'll be ready to listen to reason."

"So be it," John Alex said.

She came out of her musing temporarily – languidly opening her eyes to the strong sun. A small knot of passengers had gathered at the rail to watch the play of a pod of whales. She felt too relaxed, too involved with her reflection, to join them.

She closed her eyes again, wanting to think through further the business about Roddy. Drunk at age eighteen. That had been Neddy Gunn's problem or a good part of it – alcohol. What gets into people who can't or won't measure up? King Edward came to mind – Eddie the Quitter, he'd been called. Helped raise troop morale on the Western Front – adored by millions – yet becoming seedy with time, ab-dicating the throne of an empire for the love of an American

148

divorcee – missing his destiny. Was Roddy's life to be wasted too like Neddy Gunn's, like Edward's?

The ship changed course a few points, just enough to put her in the chill Gulf breeze. A steward came down the deck with an armful of blankets. Jessica gratefully pulled one up to her chin. The whale watchers were gone.

Neddy Gunn could have pulled back from the brink. But he wouldn't. On and on with liquor while at the same time funding Richard Bedford's bigoted fulminations. Going down the drain – down, down – until the Crash of '28 finished him.

That was a terrible day, the day Binny called to say that the bailiff put locks on the Gunn-Lawson office and only days later beautiful Craigellachie was seized and the Gunns ordered to get out in thirty days. Sad. Sad. Sad. Too much for Charlotte Gunn. Neddy so sloshed at her funeral he had to be propped up, an embarrassment to all concerned, and almost immediately after rushed to the hospital convulsed with the DTs, dying before their eviction date came due, from advanced cirrhosis of the liver.

The painful memory of it made Jessica wince and turn her closed eyes away from the sun beginning to lower over the ship's bow. What was to become of Roddy? Johnny had pinned so much on him. Was that realistic?

She felt bitter towards Joanna on this score. She kept the depth of this emotion to herself, but it was she, Joanna, who put this desire to start a family dynasty into Johnny's head. He had told her as much years before but she had thought nothing of it then. Now, for some time, the awareness of his attachment to this ambition had weighed heavily on her.

Only once had she rounded on him in anger and that

was when he fulminated against Roddy one evening after her stressful day spent at St. Christopher House. "Forget it, Johnny," she said heatedly. "Lay off, you've said enough. Water will always find its own level. Your own mother said so, and she might have gone on to say to you "what shall it profit a man if he shall gain the whole world and lose his own soul."

Having exploded, she bit her lip, knowing she had gone too far. Indeed, she had, and he barely spoke to her for a number of days. But it had the effect of dampening his criticism of the boy.

★ ★ ★

When John Alex came out of the ship's billiard saloon to join her, Jessica was sound asleep. He sat in the chair next to her looking over the gray-blue waters of the Gulf to the far-off shore, now no more than a pencil line on the fading day's horizon, yet enough to remind him of the Toronto waterfront approached by lakeboat and slowly revealing the Royal York Hotel, the Bank of Commerce and the spire of St. James Cathedral. But before all of that the sprawl of Sunnyside Amusement Park to the west near the mouth of the Humber River whose headwaters lay somewhere north of where he was born.

Sunnyside – Coney Island North – where one hot afternoon he and Noah walked and talked while Stella and Jessica sipped ginger ale in the shade. Noah that day said, "Get things into perspective, son. Don't expect the impossible of Roddy. We aren't all cut from the same cloth. Give him a longer leash. There's time."

Noah's advice. But then he, John Alex, had to lay that beside the stricture pronounced by McCaul, wiping the moisture from his forehead, standing beside the blackboard in the last days of June. "You are about to pass out of this school forever. Forever. Mark that. Forever.

"When you are young, you tend to think that life goes on and on. It doesn't. It's like the water in the Humber. It goes by only once. Make use of it. It can't be brought back, and when you go out of here to high school or to earn a living, remember that whatever success you are going to have depends on work – hard work. Nothing replaces work and remember that work keeps us from three great evils – boredom, vice and poverty."

Suddenly John Alex sat up, then stood up with the help of his cane and started back towards the billiard saloon, muttering, "How many times have I said as much to Roddy. What's the use?"

After the affair that took the Tyrones down to Niagara Falls in January, John Alex vented his displeasure on Roddy just once. It was on their way home from the police court hearing in February.

John Alex had paid the fine and damages that morning; that didn't bother him. What really bothered him was Roddy's day-by-day fecklessness – the car escapade in Tonawanda being the worst, but not the only example. He expected more of his son and heir. Much more, in spite of Jessica's talk about water finding its own level.

"Get this straight," he said. "This is the first and last time for this kind of nonsense. If there is ever anything like it again, you can stew in your own juice. Do I make myself understood? No bail. No fine payment. No damages payment. And another thing, you have to start bearing down on your school work. Tell me now that you're going to try."

"I'll try, Dad. But Dad – the accident – there was ice on the road.

"Ice be damned," said John Alex, "you were drunk."

Nothing more was said. The family was at peace. But Roddy couldn't or wouldn't apply himself at school.

It came as no surprise to either parent to learn on their return from England that he had, by his own admission, bungled his junior matriculation. "What's it to be?" asked John Alex, "go back next year or go to work?"

"Work," Roddy said without wavering.

"Then work it is – for Royal Spring or someone else?"

"Royal Spring."

"Good... good... that pleases me. Matter of fact, you can start Monday in the Queen Street store, there's an opening in the stock room.

★   ★   ★

It was while Roddy was working in the Queen Street stock room that he met Theresa Flynn.

The Flynn ancestor had immigrated to Toronto's Cabbagetown during the Irish famine. In 1919, Sergeant Desmond Flynn arrived home from overseas and soon after found employment with Hector Malloy as a chauffeur cum bodyguard. Malloy was a bootlegger, gambler and confidence man. His one honest activity, as far as anyone could tell, was his Shamrock Stud Farm which brought him international attention as a breeder of top thoroughbreds.

On November 7, 1932, the same day that Franklin Delano Roosevelt was elected thirty-second president of the United States, Flynn drove Malloy to New York City to collect some over due accounts for bootleg whiskey.

152

They didn't return. Police on both sides of the border were reluctantly alerted at the end of the month by Malloy's family. At Christmas, a New York detective, in the course of a routine investigation, came across Malloy's Packard in an unused warehouse by the East River. It was empty of all personal traces save the lingering offence of stale cigar smoke.

The men's whereabouts was never discovered. Underworld contacts led nowhere. Police dragged the East River. Nothing. Malloy and Flynn had vanished like the river's morning mist.

Flynn's disappearance left his wife Maureen destitute with four mouths to feed beside her own – Theresa, the eldest, followed by Emmett, Peter and Marilyn. With city relief she was able – barely – to survive the Depression.

The turnover in flats was constant as landlords tried frantically to get tenants who could keep up with their rent. Maureen's landlord at the time was, fortunately, an old friend of her husband. He didn't press when, of necessity, she couldn't settle at month's end.

In other times and circumstances, Theresa Flynn would have continued her education. But these were hard times. Coming home from school one afternoon in '36, she saw a sign, 'Cleaning Woman Wanted', placed prominently in the window of the Roxy's box office just minutes before. Saul Berman, the theatre's owner and manager, hired her on the spot after she lied about her age. It didn't occur to him to ask about school. As a neighbour had commented to Maureen, "She seems older than she really is."

In November, when Lillian the box office attendant took another job, Berman asked Theresa to fill the vacancy.

★ ★ ★

Roddy preferred the stock room to the class room. He mastered the parts' code quickly. There wasn't any pressure other than to arrive on time. No homework. It was a long way across the city on the streetcar, but that didn't bother him.

His co-worker was Admiral Bond – Addy to everyone. He heard Roddy yodelling *sotte voce* in the back of the stock room one day when business was slack. "Ever think of going in an amateur hour?" he asked.

"You mean like Major Bowes' Amateur Hour?" Roddy asked in turn.

"Yep. One in the Roxy down the block every week with prizes. Dames like guys that sing and dance. I'm helping Mr. Berman, the owner, to get local talent. Can I give him your name? You sound good."

Sure. Why not. What can I lose?"

"What can you win is more like it."

"Yeah, like what?"

"Like cuff links, hairbrush set, passes to Maple Leaf Gardens. Lots more."

"That all?"

"That all? D'yah think you're Wilf Carter?"

"Okay. Put my name down for a cowboy song. Keep it between us, I don't want teasing."

"Sure. Sure. Let's say you'll go by the name 'Tex' for the show. Has a real western sound."

Roddy smiled widely. "Why not?" Sure. Why not?"

★   ★   ★

Roddy's love of cowboy songs started in Humber Bend during summer holidays when he wasn't at Royal Summer.

He preferred Humber Bend where Grandma Tyrone made a lot of him, keeping the little room under the eves exclusively his — the same little room where as a boy his father used to drift into sleep, lulled by the river's murmur at the dam.

In Humber Bend, he had freedom to enjoy boyish pleasures — skinny dipping at the bridge, scoffing apples from a farmer's orchard, farting noisily. Mostly he took pleasure in learning to strum a guitar and singing cowboy songs, coached by his cousin Upton — Watt's boy.

Cowboy songs belonged to the Depression; their plaintive verses of lost love and lost occasion touched a common chord. The twangy music went with country spaces and silences, and the never to be forgotten steam whistle blowing for crossings in the distance.

Hear the train blow dear,
hear the train blow.
Late in the evening,
hear the train blow.

Sentimental twaddle to some. Food for the soul to others.

On Wednesday after work, Roddy entered the Queen City Café and ordered a western sandwich and malted milk. Addy met him there at six-thirty and they proceeded across the street to the Roxy. "This here's Tex Tyrone. He's in the amateur hour," Addy told Theresa Flynn in the box office.

"Pays twenty-five cents like everyone else," she said snapping two tickets from the roll on the counter before her.

"Okay. Okay. Just thought..."

"Don't think. That's fifty cents for the two of you."

"Got fifty cents, Tex? I'm broke 'til Friday."

* * *

Roddy was outfitted in the current costume of a cowboy singer, courtesy of Addy's brother, Commodore, who handed them a parcel out the back door of Broadway Costumes on King Street.

After the credits rolled following the end of *Lives of the Bengal Lancers*, The curtain folded across the screen and a spotlight shone on centre stage. In a black shirt, white tie and matching white shoes, Saul Berman stepped into the light and intoned, "Ladies and Gentlemen, welcome once again to another sensational hour of amateur entertainment at the Roxy."

"It better be sensational to make up for last week," a male voice shouted.

"Tonight it gives me great pleasure to introduce to you the first of our four special contestants," said Saul.

"Four too many," shouted the same heckler."

"Shut up! Get on with the show," shouted someone else.

Saul continued, "And now our first contestant this evening, Miss Dolly Brenton, the toast of Riverdale, our very own little Ginger Rogers. Give her a big hand ladies and gentlemen."

Dolly, aged twelve, tripped out on stage in a costume just like the one worn by the great Ginger in *Top Hat*. She went nimbly through her tap dance number accompanied by her older sister on the piano, then high stepped off stage twirling her cane to loud applause and whistling.

A young man in black-face doing an Al Jolson imitation sang, *Swannee* and got a good hand. Another young man, hair slicked back with brilliantine, played *Blake's March* on his accordion.

It was Roddy's turn and Saul, unlit cigar poised as

though he himself had a comic act, said, "Ladies and gentlemen, tonight for the very first time on our stage, Tex Tyrone." Roddy stepped into the spotlight, cowboy hat cocked forward. He struck a couple of chords and started into his song.

I love the open prairies
I love the coyotes wail,
rounding up the doggies
along the dusty trail,
saddling up my pony
just before the breakfast horn
Take me back to old Montana
the place where I was born.

Oh lee-lo-lo-lo-lee
Oh-lay-dee-lay-dee-dee
Oh-lee-yay-dee-loo.

As the applause died down, Roddy retreated from the stage and Saul Berman took the spotlight again. "That's it ladies and gentlemen, see you next week again when our feature film will be *Beau Geste*, starring Gary Cooper and Brian Donlevy. We will have more excellent talent in our amateur show."

"And more excellent bullfeathers from you," shouted the earlier voice from the dark.

★   ★   ★

The next day Roddy asked Addy for the name of the girl in the box office. He replied that her name was Theresa, "and a good looker, eh?"

A few days later, Roddy was in the Queen City Café when Theresa came across the street for her usual cold drink before matinee time. She sat in the window booth and ordered a lime squash. He caught her eye and when she looked away, he went over to her booth with his Coca-Cola and asked if she would mind.

"I don't mind," she said diffidently.

"Remember me?" Roddy asked as he sat facing her.

"Sure. You're Addy's pal. The cowboy. And your real name isn't Tex, is it?"

"No, maybe Addy told you, my real name is Roddy."

"That's right. And he told me your father is the boss of Royal Spring, only he hardly ever comes to the store. So you like to yodel? Can't stand it myself."

"What kind of music do you like?"

"Swing. Benny Goodman... Tommy Dorsey."

"Artie Shaw."

"Of course. He's wonderful. Has a new record that CFRB has been playing all week." She pursed her lips slightly and hummed the first bars of the song.

"Would you like to go to a dance where Artie Shaw is playing?" His eyes were imploring her.

"Would I?" her eyebrows arched quizzically.

"I've tickets. They're coming to the Palais Royale. Will you come with me?"

"Are you sure you want to ask me?"

Sure, I'm sure."

"Okay then."

Theresa fancied herself as a look-alike of the screen star Barbara Stanwyck. She did have the star's good features, but more than that, her tough directness. "Mr. Berman will have to give me the night off," she said.

"He should," said Roddy. "We're going to use my prize tickets for yodelling."

★   ★   ★

On the first Friday of September, John Alex and Jessica were finishing supper. Roddy had excused himself and gone upstairs, almost immediately coming back down and leaving by the front door.

"Where's he off to so fast?" asked John Alex.

"A dance at the Palais Royale," she replied.

"Didn't know he had a taste for that sort of thing."

"Now you do," she said, and then, "He's a bit of an enigma, that young man."

"How so?"

"Doesn't tell us much, does he. I found out this evening before supper − with a little prompting, mind you − that he has an attraction to the cashier at the Roxy Theatre near the Queen Street store. But that's only part of it, listen to this, he went into an amateur hour at the Roxy and it's as a result that he's going to the Palais Royale. He won the tickets. Not only that, Johnny, he told me his stage name is Tex. He sang a cowboy song Upton taught him."

John Alex guffawed. "Tex... Tex?"

"I thought you liked a little hillbilly music yourself, Johnny." Jessica's brown eyes were on him above an infectious smile.

"I don't want that to get around," he smiled back. "I'll say this for *Tex,* he's doing a fine job on Queen Street. I'm proud of him.

"I like to hear you say that darling. Let's finish our coffee in the living room... time for the evening news."

Switching the radio on, the first words they heard were, "It's no longer doom and gloom in the automobile industry. General Motors, Ford and Chrysler have all announced increased sales for the third quarter.

"That's music to my ears," said John Alex.

"Now from overseas," the newscaster went on. "In London, Paris and other capitals, there is mounting concern over Germany's intentions in the Sudetenland. There is a widespread pressure on leaders to get Hitler to back down. The Reuters news agency confirmed today yesterday's reports of massive German troop deployment along the north, west and southern borders with Czechoslovakia."

They sat glumly through this, barely taking in the rest of the news, until the broadcast concluded with the local news that a sentence of ten years imprisonment and twenty lashes had been handed down to a York Township rapist.

"I'm not sure that the lash is necessary," Jessica observed.

"It's a deterrent," said John Alex. And that was that, for the prospect of war was uppermost in their concern.

"You realize," he went on, "that if there is war, Canada will be pulled in and if Canada is pulled in, I'm afraid Roddy will be pulled in."

"It's bleak, very bleak, unthinkable."

"What are your lady friends saying?"

"The only one I've talked to in the past week was Rose Fine."

"And?"

"You may find this a little hard to believe. Nathan thinks that Britain and France should force Hitler to stand down."

"Stand down? That's laughable. Right now Britain and France can do no such thing thanks to the effect of pacifists

160

like Nathan. What's made him change his mind?"

"I'm not sure exactly, but both of us know that the Nazis are clamping down unmercifully on communists and Jews. Let's hope and let's pray that boys like Roddy will not have to go to war as you did."

"And as you did" He paused and then, his curiosity piqued, asked, "What are the Fines up to these days?"

"They've just moved into an apartment on Bathurst Street near St. Clair. David Fine is now managing director of the suit company.

"That suit old man Fine made for me was the best I ever had."

"Rose and Nathan are full time with the union – and also very active with the CCF."

"That's a communist outfit."

"No, Johnny. There are communists associated with it, but it's not a communist outfit, as you call it. It's a bona fide party, similar to the Labour Party in Britain. However, you and Nathan will be divided on this..."

"We're divided on a lot of things."

"Nathan is quite angry about the Premier's strike-breaking tactics at General Motors."

"Well, he would be, wouldn't he? He can think what he likes. Hepburn did the right thing. Absolutely the right thing. The UAW-CIO and their agitators are going to destroy us if they are not stopped."

"You really think so, don't you Johnny?"

"Yes, dammit, I do. General Motors may be able to handle John L. Lewis and his thugs – but we can't."

"Darling, that's a bridge we'll have to cross when we come to it."

"God forbid."

"What do you say to an early bedtime?" she asked, and smiling she stood up, kissed him lightly on the forehead and started for the staircase.

★   ★   ★

At the end of September, news of the Munich Pact reached Canada by radio. "Prime Minister Neville Chamberlain declares it is peace in our time. Britain and Germany won't be going to war."

In Toronto, summer lingered. Downtown, Allan Gardens was an island of well-shaded green, a retreat for the down and out drawn from their nearby lodgings; a place to sit, to stroll, to read, to watch, to play checkers, to argue with others... On Sunday afternoons, its population swelled as people from farther out arrived to enjoy the fauna in the great glass house or to hear one of the many soapbox preachers under the trees.

"In Europe, you can be shot for saying what you think." the young speaker had the attention of his small audience. "...there's France... there's Mussolini... There's Hitler..."

"What about Duplessis?" a stocky man, fedora square on his brow, called out.

"Yeah, what about Duplessis?" echoed someone further back.

"What about Duplessis and his bloody Padlock Act? He's another damn dictator."

"Please," a young man in clerical collar turned in the direction of this last intervention. He was with three other well-dressed young people. "Please," he repeated, "there are ladies here."

The offender reddened and in a voice meant to carry said to his grinning neighbour, "Well whaddaya think of that? Whaddaya think of that? more concerned with a little cuss word than fascism."

The other young man on the wooden stand continued. "Now, friends, let me pose a question to you. Does anyone believe that the deal with Hitler, signed by Chamberlain, is anything more than a worthless scrap of paper?"

"As worthless as an Eaton's catalogue in an outhouse," someone quipped.

"Wrong friend," shot back the young speaker, who fancied his own wit. "An Eaton's catalogue in an outhouse does serve one purpose."

"That's it," said a professional type in horn-rimmed glasses. "That's it. The Munich Pact, an Eaton's catalogue in an outhouse, that outhouse being Europe right now. Perfect metaphor."

"Can we get back on topic?" the young cleric asked.

Roddy and Theresa had come along, hand in hand, just in time to hear the Pact referred to as an Eaton's catalogue. "Dad says Chamberlain is playing a fool's game," said Roddy, trying to keep his voice low enough to not draw attention.

"Does he?" she asked, attempting to sound interested.

"Yeah. Dad says if you're going to eat with the devil, you'd better use a long spoon."

"That sounds like Father O'Malley."

"Father O'Malley?"

"Yes, our priest."

"What Dad means is you can't trust Hitler. He's going to drag us into a war." Now he had her full attention.

"Will you go if they have a war? Our grocer, Mr.

Shannon is still getting shrapnel out of his back from the Great War."

"I know about shrapnel. Dad took me into Christie Street Hospital to see an old friend from the War and I saw it for myself. Dad himself almost lost a leg in the War. Can't go anywhere without a cane."

"I want to meet your mother and father, cowboy."

"Sure."

"When?"

"When? I'll ask Mom — next Sunday most likely. That okay?"

"Very okay."

As Roddy stretched out a motor rug in an empty patch of shade, the Salvation Army band, just entering the Gardens on the Jarvis Street side, struck up 'Land of Hope and Glory'.

And if there's a war, you'll go?"

"Maybe there won't be a war."

"I didn't ask that."

"Maybe."

- 1939 -

The peace bubble broke a year later. Germany marched into Poland. Britain and France declared war. Canada followed suit.

The considerations behind Canada's declaration of war, touted in government pronouncements and newspaper editorials, did not directly influence Roddy's decision to join the army. For him the war represented an opportunity to bust out of the chrysalis of home, humdrum work, even his affair with Theresa, which was, yes, sexually stimulating and tender, but also cloying. He wanted space – a larger air to breathe. And wasn't it admirable to do something brave – something to raise yourself in the eyes of father, mother, sweetheart, aunts and uncles, co-workers, neighbours?

"I'm going to sign up," he told Bert Powell, the Queen Street store manager. "I'm old enough."

"How old is that."

"Twenty last January."

"And what does your old man think?"

"Haven't told him – or Mom. Don't you tell them. They'll find out soon enough."

"And how soon would that be?"

"Tonight."

After lunch, he drove to the Exhibition grounds and queued at the recruiting office of the Royal Regiment of Canada. "It used to be Dad's old Toronto Regiment," he explained later to those who asked, "Why the Royal Regiment?"

The enlistment procedure was speedy. In a matter of a few short hours, he passed a medical examination, swore allegiance to King George VI, indicated his next of kin, drew his kit and was assigned a cot in one of the Exhibition buildings, still pungent with the lingering smell of horse.

All of this was at a time when his attentions had brought Theresa to the point where she was fantasizing about marriage. Her priest, Father O'Malley, would uphold church law – for sure. That was Deirdre McGrath's experience, her girlfriend. Deirdre was engaged to a Protestant boy but the combined pressure from Father O'Malley and the boy's stubborn mother was too much and they broke off their engagement.

The priest would insist on talks with Roddy, urging him to 'turn', or at the very least consent to have the children of the union baptized and raised as Catholics. Roddy himself was indifferent, this she knew. But his parents?

She didn't like to remember the Sunday she was introduced to the Tyrones, the year before. Would they try to block a marriage?

"This is my mother, Theresa," – he usually called her Tess.

"Glad to meet you, Mrs. Tyrone."

"And I to meet you, Theresa", as they shook hands.

Then the polite exchange of greetings with John Alex and the MacLarens.

"Sit anywhere you will be comfortable," said Jessica, the good hostess.

She chose a brocaded straight-back, sitting stiffly, legs placed discretely before her, hands overlapped on her knees exactly as she had been instructed by the nuns to sit for her first communion.

"What can I offer you to drink? Sherry... root beer?" Jessica asked.

Theresa looked at Roddy, perched on the piano bench, unlit cigarette held stylishly and replied, "Root beer, please."

"Teh-ree-suh" sounded Amy meditatively from the chesterfield. "I know a Theresa... Theresa Quinn on Quebec Avenue. Pretty name. The Quinns go to St. Cecilia's Catholic Church on Annette Street."

"Theresa *is* a Catholic," said Roddy. "Her father was a sergeant in the war."

This information prompted a silence and some shifting in their seats. Amy's gaze was fixed out the window as though there had been an accident in the street. "A sergeant, eh?" said John Alex. "What regiment would that be?" He was leaning slightly forward, both hands on his cane, and she replied, "The Irish Regiment, sir, the Irish Regiment of Toronto."

John Alex, like his family for generations, was Protestant to the bone, although he never joined the Orange Order. As for Jessica, her outlook, liberal and all as it was, did not encompass the idea that her only son might some day marry a Catholic.

Theresa remembered that day as something unreal. Surface civility. Awkward silences. Grateful farewells. From

167

that time it was obvious to her that if her relationship with Roddy was to develop in the direction of marriage, she would have to be patient and play out her line a long way in order to catch him. But somehow, steering a course between the Scylla of Father O'Malley and the Charybdis of the senior Tyrones, she meant to reach her goal.

"What are the Tyrones like?" her mother asked.

"They're kind of stuck-up Maw."

"Whaddaya mean, stuck-up? Because they're rich, is that it?"

"Naw, not that?"

"Well whaddaya saying?"

"I'm saying because they're Protestant they're stuck-up."

"I'll be damned. And I suppose they think they can get to heaven on that ticket. What about Roddy? He doesn't give himself airs now, does he?"

"Naw."

"And what about you? It's time you dropped him and found a nice Catholic boy."

"Can't, he's got under my skin."

"You want to marry him?"

"Yes, I do, yes."

"I thought as much. And what about religion? What about their birth control? What about Father O'Malley?"

"Slow up, Maw. I'll cross those bridges when I get to them."

"You know what I think? I think you ought to go to confession before this affair goes any further."

"For what sin, Maw? What sin?"

★   ★   ★

Roddy was starting a hamburger when Saul Berman stepped into the Queen City Café for his usual corn beef on rye. He eased himself onto the seat opposite.

"You look older, cowboy, with a uniform."

"There's a war, Mr. Berman."

"I know. I know. You should tell me? Saw Hitler's *blitzkrieg* in the newsreel last night. People didn't even know that word a month ago. That bastard is mopping up Poland."

"He'll get what's coming to him."

"You're taking Tess home tonight?"

"Yep. I've a weekend pass – maybe take a run out to Sunnyside tomorrow...

★   ★   ★

Sunnyside was a disappointment. Most of the amusements had closed. There was a sharp breeze from the lake and they got back in the car.

"Where to?" asked Roddy.

"Isn't there some place we can ride and talk?"

"Sure."

They drove west on Lakeshore Road, silent as far as New Toronto where Theresa broached what for her was uppermost.

"You'll write me often?"

"Hey – who knows when I'll be leaving Toronto."

"Yeah, but sooner or later, you'll be going, that's for sure – the war's not in Toronto."

"Okay, sure, I'll be writing you often from wherever I'll be when the regiment is ordered out."

"You and me Roddy – we been on a merry-go-round

169

of walks and talks and dances for a year. When are we getting married? Or are you the marrying kind?"

Roddy braked and pulled to a stop by the curb outside the Goodyear Tire factory. Facing her, his arm behind her shoulders, he pulled her to him and kissed her passionately.

"That's my answer," he said. "I love you and I want to marry you."

She straightened her little hat and through her smeared lipstick said, "That's what I want too, cowboy."

They drove on without speaking, full of the urge to hold one another. At last, Roddy stopped at the edge of a quiet side road. Autumn's dusk was upon them, advanced by the farmer's tall wood lot. For some time they sat quietly, his hand on her skirt above the knee, her head on his shoulder. Day was fading when as one and as though propelled by an invisible hand, they got out of the car with the car blanket – the same one they had put down a year before on the shaded grass of Allan Gardens – now stretching it in a slight depression beside the fence line. And here, in the dying day, they stretched out, body to body, lip to lip, oblivious to all else but the moment's sweetness.

★   ★   ★

After enlisting, Roddy was in Toronto a full eight months doing basic training. Two, three times a week he arrived at Flynns' on Shuter Street, never empty handed. The children looked forward to these visits – these treats of apples or ice cream – maybe a cake.

Arriving one Saturday, while on a weekend pass, he overheard Maureen as he went up the porch steps talking to the neighbour next door. "They're going to start rationing fuel and food, that's a laugh. We already have rationing only we call it City relief."

"Won't mean a thing, not a blessed thing," said the neighbour, "but maybe it'll smarten up some people in Rosedale with two cars and the like."

Running the Flynn household was a harrowing balancing act that showed in Maureen's pinched face and in the premature graying of her lustrous red hair. How many times had she been in the gas company's office to pay her arrears after they'd been cut off by the accounts' department? She couldn't remember. Then she couldn't pay the landlord. The landlord paid, then she couldn't pay the hydro. The hydro paid, then the gentle Mr. Shannon was cleaning his throat, "God bless you Mrs. Flynn, do you not think you can pay down your account at least a little, I have my own bills to pay you see."

"Yes, yes Mr. Shannon, I see. Of course, you have your own bills. I'll try. God bless you too Mr. Shannon. Can you fix me up in the meantime with some flour and potatoes and tea? I am grateful to you, Mr. Shannon, you have always been very understanding."

Notwithstanding his soldiering and her job at the box office, Roddy and Theresa had many dates in that eight months between September 1939 and April 1940, almost invariably walking somewhere or roller skating at Mutual Street Arena or simply sipping Coca-Cola at the Queen City Café.

They hadn't consummated their passion beside the farmer's woodcut, but the urge was constantly there and but for Theresa's fear of an unmarried pregnancy, they could easily have given way. She willed by thought and prayer to hold the course all the way to the alter. That involved among other things, keeping on an even keel with Maureen, Father O'Malley and, of course, the Tyrones..

★   ★   ★

More often than not, Roddy experienced a surging tumescence when he was with Theresa; thus he frequently returned to barracks with a painful groin. In their bawdy talk, his regimental mates described this condition as 'lover's nuts' which, according to them wasn't a problem if you took advantage of the free condoms issued by the medical officer.

On fire with passion, one night when they were rubbing against each other on the front walk before saying goodnight, Roddy gently mentioned to Theresa, as if she didn't know, the way pregnancy could be avoided, other than by continence. She shoved him away angrily, "Intercourse is for marriage, cowboy, *without* using Frenchies. Using those things is a sin."

She could have repeated to him a pithy lecture recently delivered to her by Maureen who heard that 'used' condoms were found lying around on the grass in Exhibition Park every morning. "A Jarvis Street whore might allow those things, but *you*, never. Get it, *never*. It's a sin on top of the sin of laying with a man before you marry."

Maureen pressed the point repeatedly that Theresa and Roddy get engaged immediately and set a wedding date to which Theresa would reply, "It's going to happen, Maw. It's going to happen."

And it did happen or started to happen, on Easter Monday in the Tyrone living room while John Alex and Jessica were visiting the Oldfields and the maid, Doreen, had the day off. Roddy slipped the engagement ring on her third finger, left hand. And then, there in mid-room they kissed, clung to each other, careening all the while across the room to the chesterfield where the flood gates of their pent up passion finally gave way.

★   ★   ★

Maureen was ecstatic when that same evening Theresa gave her the news of the wedding engagement. But next day, encountering Father O'Malley, as she came out of Shannon's Grocery, her pleasure was dampened by his poker-faced reaction and caution that, "the couple need to take time. The boy doesn't know the first thing about his responsibilities in marrying a Catholic." Which wasn't exactly the case, for Theresa had coached Roddy for some months.

A few days later, Roddy told John Alex and Jessica. They put on a good act of being pleased. But not to seem too quick, Jessica waited until after supper to ask, "Don't you think you should hold off, dear, until the war's over, for both your sakes."

John Alex quickly added, "I'm with your mother on this, a war creates widows and orphans."

The next morning Theresa told Roddy in the Queen City Café, "Father O'Malley doesn't think it's a good think, under the circumstances, for us to tie the knot just now."

"Yeah, maybe it's the best thing for the time, until the war is over, won't be long," he responded – not wishing to implicate his parents.

The regiment moved from Toronto to Camp Borden in mid-April, and from there in June to Halifax for embarkation to Iceland.

★   ★   ★

The Royals were days at sea when Theresa had her first real bout of morning sickness. On that same day, she went and had her pregnancy confirmed at St. Michael's Hospital. She told Maureen who was predictably furious. "What did I tell you... what did I tell you?" she screamed, "them that plays with fire get burned."

Her attitude softened a few days later after talking to Father O'Malley whom she waylaid at the door of the sacristy after early mass. "It's happened, Father," she said.

"What's happened?"

"Theresa, she's pregnant by that Protestant soldier."

"I'm truly sorry," the priest responded, although he already knew from Theresa's visit to the confessional. "It could have been... should have been different."

"What now, Father? Will the Church forgive her?"

"Of course, of course, my daughter. We can't lock people away from the presence of God – there's always a way home through true penitence."

"Thank you, Father. I'm so relieved."

"What's important now is that we prepare for the safe arrival of the child and strengthen Theresa to stand by her Catholic faith."

"Yes, Father."

With a long day ahead in one of Canada's poorest parishes, and hungry for breakfast, the priest excused himself, saying, "We'll talk again soon," as he moved into the sacristy and closed the door.

★   ★   ★

Exposed to Iceland's frequent rain and high winds, the Royals hardened up doing road, airfield and tank trap construction – not to the neglect of daily small arms training. In the evening, some roistered with the native rotgut dubbed, "Black Death."

Roddy was half expecting Theresa's news when it arrived in the regimental post, but he had pushed the possibility of pregnancy to the back of his mind after their engagement day. That evening he got drunk and had to be assisted back to barracks. A few days later, he wrote Theresa saying that things would work out when he got home and enclosed five dollars.

★   ★   ★

In early December, Theresa left work to await the natal day. Saul Berman told her not to worry, that his wife, Golda would fill in and just to look after herself.

On the evening of December 8, the Feast of the Immaculate Conception, Maureen with Emmett, Peter and Marilyn were at Mass when Theresa, who stayed home, suddenly had a gripping cramp. She threw on her coat and, not bothering with galoshes, rushed to the emergency at St. Michael's Hospital.

When Maureen and family reached home, the front door was ajar. She knew instantly that Theresa had left for St. Michael's. Shouting over her shoulders that Emmett put coal in the heater, she was off the porch in a flash and, out of breath, arrived a few minutes later at the hospital. Theresa was already in the delivery room. At ten o'clock, a young doctor with a smile came out to the corridor where she was standing and said that it was a boy – a healthy, seven pound boy.

175

Theresa wrote Roddy on December 14.

Dear Roddy,

You became a father to a healthy boy on December 8, our Christmas present to each other. He hasn't much hair just a little fuzz and I love his little fingers. I've decided to call him Royal. Made up my mind about that back in the summer that if it was a boy it was going to be Royal because that will always remind me about you without giving anything away. Royal is good enough a name for your father's company and it's good enough for the Royal Regiment. I even went to the phone book in Mr. Berman's office and there are lots of Royals. It's a very popular name and classy like Royal Winter Fair, Royal Carpet Cleaners, Royal Bank, Royal Canadian Mounted Police and lots more at least a full page. Don't worry, your folks don't know about Roy — that's what I'm going to call him every day — and they won't unless someone over at your store blabs and I don't think they will because I'm never around there and Addy has joined the navy he is now an admiral, ha! ha! Anyway, thank you for your last letter and another five dollars like you sent from Iceland and telling me about the big mascot you have Lance-Private Royal. I once saw a Saint-Bernard in a newsreel helping get people out of a snow pile. Father O'Malley and the sisters at St. Michael's want me to give Roy to the Catholic Children's Aid for adoption. I'll die first. Hope you feel the same way cowboy.

Yours forever,

Theresa

xxxooo

*   *   *

Theresa's arrival home with Roy went almost unnoticed on hard-bitten Shuter Street except for a very few dry comments between neighbours on the street and in Shannon's Grocery store.

The war made no difference to the poverty of the Flynn household – a situation of which Father O'Malley was painfully aware. He was ground down by the bottomless pit of need around him and he often did without in order to help in the parish. His housekeeper, Mrs. Moore, would say, "Father, there was a case of beans in the pantry just yesterday." And he would reply, "Was there now, Mrs. Moore, I don't recall." And she would walk away, hands raised once again to the silent ceiling.

When the temperature plunged to zero in January, he thought particularly of the Flynns and the baby. In the dark before early mass, he fetched two brimming sacks of coal to the Flynn porch in the back seat of his old Chev. Later, if any in the congregation noticed that he lifted the Host and Chalice with soot smudged wrists, they didn't comment.

In mid-January, Teresa went back to work. It meant that Saul Berman was again free to puff cigars in the office, banned while Golda was standing in at the box office.

He was just in the process of lighting one when Theresa came to the door in tears, a half-hour before the box office opened for the afternoon matinee. "Hey, what's the matter kid?" he asked.

"The landlord's demanding his rent or he's putting us on the street," she sobbed. "Can you give me a loan on my pay?"

Saul was raised in the Spadina Jewish district, no stranger to the humiliation imposed by poverty. "You don't want a loan Tess," he said. "Wipe your tears, I'll look after it, today yet."

An hour later, he drove to Shuter Street and banged on the front door. Maureen heard him from the back where she was hanging wash. She opened the front door with reddened hands. He said, "I'm Saul Berman."

"Yes, I've seen you on Queen Street, Theresa likes working for you."

"Well now," said Saul, somewhat taken off guard, "that a fact. You wonder why I'm here? Tess says you can't pay your rent. I know the feeling. Can you do me a favour? Send the collector over to me. I won a little money last week at poker. It oughta be enough to take care of a couple of months until you get straightened out."

She was dumbstruck but managed a thin smile and a thank you, raising the corner of her apron to dry her eyes.

"It's okay. I know you're doing everything you can," Saul said, sharing her embarrassment.

- 1942 -

Royal Flynn was a year and eight months when the father he would never see was killed in action at Dieppe on August 19, 1942.

Just days before that, the Royal Spring and Axle Company finally got its new wartime subsidiary into production in Weston. The sign beside the double front door read, Royal Spring Projectile Works. It was there that Jessica reached John Alex by phone. "Come home, Johnny. Come now. There's a telegram from National Defence," and she hung up.

She was sitting on the front room chesterfield, motionless, the telegram in her lap, when he came in and sat beside her. He took it, knowing full well the gist of its content – *regret to inform – killed in action – raid in Dieppe.* A numbing sensation covered his forehead and suddenly he was very thirsty. "Can Doreen bring us something to drink?" he asked, and to Jessica his pallor suggested more than mere thirst. Out in the kitchen she found Doreen sobbing as she rolled pastry. She got the drinks herself.

All along they had feared it would come to this, going from day to day on tenterhooks, yet hoping. After all, the odds against their own return from the earlier war had been just as great. Now all hope was snatched from them by this piece of paper from the Defence Department.

Jessica was too numb to think of anything. But in John Alex there was a fury. Immediately his mind raced back to some lines memorized in his entrance year at Humber Bend. McCaul, posing before the senior class like a Roman senator, had introduced them as an example of the difference between an elegy and a lament. The week before he had given an exposition on Gray's *Elegy Written in a Country Churchyard*.

"Remember Absalom's rebellion against David. Remember Joab finishing Absalom off with three darts thrust into his heart. Remember David's grief when he heard of his son's death. He was deeply moved, he went up to the chamber over the grate, and wept, and as he went he said, 'O my son Absalom, my son Absalom, my son, my son Absalom! Would God I had died for thee, O Absalom, my son, my son!' I want you to memorize that verse seniors. It's called a lament. It is the music of grief... the poetry of grief... coming straight from the heart."

John Alex was suddenly off the chesterfield and staggering in the middle of the room. "Roddy, Roddy my son, my son Roddy," he moaned.

In an instant, Jessica was beside him, steadying him, kissing his moist cheek. "Go on, cry Johnny, cry, men can cry. You need to cry."

They tossed and turned and said little when they went to bed. John Alex finally dozed off after downing the heel of a twenty-six of rye, but Jessica settled on a glass of warm milk with the same effect.

The next morning had to be faced, and they dreaded it. Their world was on a different course than it had been just twenty-four hours earlier. But nothing could be gained by putting their heads in the sand.

Jessica's phone call caught Noah dozing in his armchair. "We'll be right over," was all he said, after a momentary pause.

John Alex phoned the plant to say he wouldn't be in. Minutes later he was called by Darcy Adams, Vice-President in charge of overall operations.

"Anything we need to know, J.A.?"

"Yes, Darcy, Roddy got it at Dieppe." The line went silent. Darcy Adams' own son was overseas. Finally he said, "I'm very sorry, J.A.," and then when nothing else came to mind he added, "Anything I can do?"

"Just hold on for a day or so until we get straightened out around here."

"Of course, J.A. Please convey my deepest sympathy to Mrs. Tyrone.

★ ★ ★

"What next?" John Alex asked Jessica.

"There's Theresa," she said. "I've put a number of calls to her since Johnny went overseas, none of them returned. There's a message in that I think."

"There is. But like it or not, they are engaged and Roddy has never said otherwise – that it was broken off."

She reached Saul Berman just as he was glancing at the front page of the Star's noon edition.

"Can I speak to Theresa Flynn?"

"Well I'm not sure where to find her just now."

"You *must* right now. It's about Roddy. It's urgent."

"Okay, okay," he said. "I'll do my best."

Minutes later Theresa called, "You have something urgent about Roddy," she said in a flat voice.

"Theresa, there's bad news for us all. Roddy was killed in the Dieppe raid. Are you there Theresa?"

"I'm here. We were going to get married. We loved each other... She couldn't continue. Jessica was left with the sounds of her low wailing and then Saul came on the line.

"She can't say any more, Mrs. Tyrone. This is a very sad day for all of us."

"I understand," said Jessica, barely containing her own grief, then tremulously adding, "Thanks Mr. Berman. You know where we are."

By this time, Theresa was running west on Queen Street to the church where she knelt, sobbing, for more than an hour.

Oldfields arrived at the Tyrone house. Doreen brought coffee to the front room.

"Bloody war," said Noah.

"He did his duty," said Stella.

Their own experience had taught them the limit of words to comfort in times of grief. The less said the better. For the moment it was their presence – their presence in love – that mattered and comforted.

★   ★   ★

In the following weeks, work held the Tyrones' grief at bay. The manager of a war plant had incessant demands on his time with innumerable meetings, and Jessica continued her volunteer work at St. Christopher House and allowed herself, with a shove from Stella, to be a candidate for membership in the Imperial Order of the Daughters of the Empire. A certain cachet attached to the mother of a son killed in action and wife of someone with John Alex' stature. Her charm and speaking ability were soon recognized. She became a coveted speaker for her own, and other chapter meetings.

In those weeks and months, their lives were like ships passing in the night. Other than Sundays they were rarely able to eat meals together. John Alex frequently took the overnight train to Ottawa for meetings with officials at the Department of Munitions and Supply – the same hard-eyed coterie who had called Royal Projectiles into being – who demanded rigorously detailed reports on all aspects of shell casing production and shipments. Any failure to meet shipping deadlines or production targets was severely questioned since Ottawa had to mesh production and transportation, coast to coast. They demanded a superhuman effort, which necessary as it had to be, didn't lessen the exasperation of managers in John Alex' position. When a particularly blunt demand arrived by courier one morning, he pounded the desk and said to Darcy Adams, "Hells bells, those bastards expect us to walk on water."

- 1944 -

On Roy's fourth birthday, Saul arrived early with a present. He found Theresa, Maureen and Roy in the front room. Something had been going on between them and they greeted him with forced smiles.

"What's wrong?" he asked.

"Nothing," Jessica answered.

"Yes there is." Maureen said.

"There is or there isn't," said Saul.

"There is," said Maureen.

"And?" asked Saul.

"We ain't got room in this flat for the bunch of us, so Theresa is going to move out and then I'll only have relief money." Maureen dabbed at her eyes with the corner of her apron. Theresa stared blankly at Roy playing with a toy on the cracked linoleum.

Saul, suddenly remembering why he came, went over to Roy and handed him his present. Roy was ecstatic. Tearing off the blue tissue wrapping, he uncovered a toy roadster made of hard rubber – a thing of beauty, fire engine red, Donald Duck at the wheel. In a trice he was running it along the floor simulating the noise of the rent collector's Ford V-8. Vroom, vroom.

"What do you say, Roy?" Maureen tried to reach him over the sound of the imaginary engine.

"Yes, what do you say Roy?" Theresa echoed, only louder.

He turned his blond head upwards. "Thank you, Mr. Berman," he said, and instantly re-focused on giving Donald Duck a spin in the red roadster.

Saul smiled, then looking at the women finding momentary relief in Roy's fun, said, "Cheer up. Maybe we can untangle this."

After he left, Theresa was on pins and needles. What did Saul mean? That afternoon she went through the Roxy's lobby to Saul's office a half-hour before the box office opened. Saul was just in the act of lighting a cigar.

"What have you in mind, Mr. Berman about un-tangling?" she asked.

He squinted at her through a cloud of smoke. "There's something that's possible. Just possible," he answered. "Give me a couple of days. Don't do anything rash."

It was three days later, actually, when Saul was admitted to the Flynn flat in mid-morning. Nothing had changed from his previous call. Peter and Sheila were at school and Emmett, turned sixteen, was delivering groceries for Shannon. They were in the front room again; Roy racing his new roadster around the floor. Maureen brought Saul a mug of tea from the pot they were just draining. "Black or white?" she asked, and he answered, "Black, no sugar." He sat cradling the mug in his hands, until Maureen took the hint and excused herself. After a further silence, he put the question to Theresa that had been bothering him. "Tell me, Tess, Roddy's family, do they know?"

"Know what?"

"About Roy."

"No."

"No?"

"I said no."

"Okay.

Why?"

"I don't want them moving in. Roy is mine."

"Roy is yours, okay, but they could help with some moola."

"Let's just keep them out of this."

"Do you think that is fair? He *is* their grandson."

"Things are better as they are."

"Have it your way."

"Drink you tea, it's getting cold."

Getting up, he gave Roy's head a pat and on his way out said over his shoulder, "Come in tomorrow morning at ten. I've an old friend I want you to meet."

She arrived at ten on the dot to find a slender man sitting across the desk from Saul in overcoat and scarf, holding an inverted fedora in his hand.

"This is the girl I want you to meet," said Saul. Nathan Fine turned a little and without standing said, "How d'uh do," to Theresa who said the same to him.

"Mr. Fine here has a position that just might be to your liking," said Saul. "He and his wife are opening a china shop on the Danforth. Rose, that's his wife, will manage it. We go back a long way, Nathan and Rose and me and Golda, and I've told him you are just the kind of clerk they need. They'll do the square thing by you." Theresa almost said, "But I don't know anything about china." Nathan stood and handed her one of their freshly printed cards:

Rose Fine China and Silverware
55 Danforth Avenue
Open Mon-Thurs 9-6, Fri 9-9, Sat 9-noon

"Do you think you can start at nine on Monday? he asked.

"Go ahead, we'll manage here," said Saul.

"Okay. I'll be there," she said, breaking into a pleased smile. In turn, Nathan flashed her one of his rare smiles and said, "Good," then turning to Saul, "Appreciate your interest, my friend. I'll be on my way, we're unpacking crates."

Nathan was already in the lobby and Saul shouted after him, "You won't regret it." Theresa went behind the desk and kissed Saul on the cheek. "You're not only a good boss, Mr. Berman, you're a good friend," she said.

The flat above Shannon's Grocery was vacant. Theresa moved in that weekend. Saul furnished it with the help of Golda and some Queen Street second hand stores. It was an ideal location, handy for Maureen to carry-on babysitting Roy.

Nathan controlled his curiosity about the arrangement. He was busy anyway negotiating with Women's World Hosiery on Spadina. Rose came into Blitstein's Delicatessen to join him after work. Waiting for their corned-beef-on-rye, she smiled at him and said, "Smart for a goy, Theresa."

"Smart for a goy," he repeated. "You like her?"

"Yeah, guess I do. She's got one hell of a figure. Men buy something every time they come in."

Christmas Eve, Rose gave Theresa an illustrated book

on English china and a bonus cheque for twenty-five dollars. That was the Christmas of 1944 and the war that claimed Roddy Tyrone two years before was winding down.

- 1947 -

Father O'Malley united Addy Bond and Theresa Flynn in Holy Matrimony in the hot summer of 1947. "Is your Christian name really Admiral?" the priest asked when they were signing the church register.

Addy answered, "I'd just as soon it didn't get out, Father, if you don't mind."

After his discharge from the Navy in early '46, Addy was re-employed by the Royal Spring and Axle Parts store on Queen Street East, where he stayed for a few months until landing a better job with the Canadian Tire store on Yonge Street. They kept Theresa's flat, for Addy didn't own a stick. Pooling their incomes meant Theresa could replace the old refrigerator installed by Saul Berman two years before.

Some days after their wedding – they couldn't afford a honeymoon – Addy said to Theresa, "I think Roddy is happy, wherever he is, that I'm with you and Roy."

"You know what Roddy thinks, do you?"

"Sure, he and me were pals."

"Yeah, you were pals and you put him up to that Tex act."

"How come you haven't told Roddy's parents about Roy? There's some talk about that."

"That's my problem and don't talk about it again to me or anyone else – okay."

"Okay, okay, just asking."

Theresa never felt about Addy the way she had for Roddy, but she did have a real affection for him, put to the test only occasionally when he drank until closing time with his pals in the men's beer parlour of the Broadview Hotel. Twice, in their first year of marriage, the police of 51 Division brought him home staggering drunk.

- 1949 -

Saul Berman held on at the Roxy until '48, when failing health forced him to sell. In January '49, he was admitted to the Wellesley Hospital and started on radiation therapy for a spreading cancer. "I miss a good cigar," he told Theresa and Addy, who visited him faithfully on most Saturday afternoons, "but that's life."

Shortly before he died, Golda was in the room beside him when they arrived. He was barely able to recognize them and Golda signalled for them to go out in the hall where she joined them. "The pain is god awful," she said, "they're not giving him any more radiation. Addy do you mind if Theresa and I have a few moments alone?"

"Sure," said Addy, moving down the hall.

Looking intently at her, Golda said to Theresa, "Saul wants to know – how is Roy taking to Addy?"

"They're okay. They weren't at first, but now Addy is doing a lot with him – playing handball on the school wall and lots of cribbage at home."

"Thanks," said Golda, "Saul was really concerned. He'll be relieved. Means a lot to him. I'll tell him."

Saul's death, two weeks later, shook Theresa as nothing had since Roddy was killed in action seven years before.

★   ★   ★

The good relationship between Rose Fine and Theresa continued. Monday mornings, Theresa arrived at the store just before nine and immediately went out with a broom to sweep the weekend litter off the sidewalk. Rose arrived sometime later.

The stock now included – in addition to china, crystal and silverware – imported linen tablecloths and napkins. The Rose Fine China catalogue, which had started as a two-page brochure, had grown to sixteen pages. On the bottom of the cover, featuring a Royal Doulton tea setting in colour, was a statement in curlicued script: "We stock over thirty names and many more patterns in fine china. *What we don't stock, we will cheerfully order and safely deliver to your address with minimum delay.*" The first week of December, Rose said to Theresa, "It's time to do our windows for the Season." She wasn't comfortable with the word Christmas.

"Do you want me to do them again this year, Mrs. Fine?" "Why not," said Rose – not a question, but her way of saying yes. Theresa enjoyed the challenge posed by the artful use of crepe paper and ribbon; of festooning with cotton batting snow the tiny Swiss houses brought out only at Christmas and placed daintily between soup tureens, tea pots, cups and saucers, on gold-laminated boxes. A card was then balanced in front of a full set of Booth's Blue Willow with the prices of some of the store's current stock.

She was putting the final touch to the first of the two windows flanking the entrance, when she became conscious of a smartly-dressed older woman holding a leather purse and staring down through the glass at the price list.

Jessica Tyrone had come to the Rose Fine China Store as the result of a chance encounter with Nathan Fine. He was on the northbound Bathurst streetcar when she got on at Dundas Street.

"It's been a long time," he said.

"A very long time," she agreed. "How's Rose? Still has her china store?"

"She does. Going well. Why don't you drop by. She has an excellent stock and she'd like to see you again."

They sat in silence past College Street as far as Harbord Street. She said, "I suppose you're still with the union."

"Still with the union," he replied. "You'd be surprised or maybe you wouldn't, at the way employers sweat immigrants. Hasn't changed much over the years."

She looked at him defensively. It bothered her deeply that John Alex had been successful in frustrating union attempts to organize the workers of Royal Spring and Axle. But now she found herself saying, "Johnny doesn't sweat anyone; tries to keep the labour code and pays the union levels." He smiled at her, a little sardonically, and said, "I'm sure he does," and she realized, with a twinge of regret as they parted at Bloor Street, how time and circumstance had distanced them from one another.

★   ★   ★

Jessica stepped briskly through the door to where Rose was bent behind a showcase rearranging things. Straightening up, she said, "Hello, hello. It's Jessica Tyrone – none other."

195

Jessica smiled warmly and said, "Hello, Rose. Long time no see."

Rose smiled too.

"Long time no see. You've put on weight, but hey! – haven't we all."

Theresa almost fell into the window at the sound of Jessica's name. Rose said, "Come over here, Theresa. I want you to meet an old friend – went to university with Nathan. How many years ago was that?" Theresa stepped over to Jessica and said, "Remember me, Mrs. Tyrone? – Theresa Flynn." Jessica felt herself tightening and her heart pound. It took her a long moment and then she said, "Theresa, it's been a lifetime. I'm glad you're working for my old friends, the Fines." Rose took this in, straining to understand.

"You two know each other, Barbara Stanwyck and Lady Astor?"

"It's not complicated, Rose. Theresa was engaged to our son."

"You mean, Roy's..." But before she could go on, Theresa squeezed hard on her elbow.

"She means, Roddy. He was killed at Dieppe. I only stopped wearing his ring just before I came to work here."

"I know, I know," said Rose, suddenly understanding Theresa's game.

"And I remember you telling me all about your soldier boy and how he liked to sing western songs. I never made any connection. How could I? You're very tight-lipped, you are, Theresa."

Tears had come into Jessica's eyes and Theresa guiltily impaled on her secret, moved away from Rose to attend to a customer who had just come in.

"Worth her weight in gold, that girl," said Rose in an undertone.

"Married a veteran in '47 – or was it '48 – doesn't matter. She's now Mrs. Bond." "I'm happy to hear that," said Jessica, also in an undertone.

"Do they have any children?"

"A boy."

"A boy?"

"I said a boy, but I don't know anything about him," Rose lied.

Jessica felt like pursuing that, but held her tongue. They stood for a time facing each other across the showcase. Finally, Jessica broke the silence, "You've a very fine place here, Rose. I'm looking for something in bone china or possibly crystal for a friend."

Rose pointed out the possible choices and Jessica finally decided on a Royal Doulton figurine. "For you, it's at cost only," said Rose. "I'm very pleased you took the trouble to come all this way, I'll tell Nathan."

Driving home, Jessica tried to put together her impressions. Something had been left unsaid. But what? Was it simply the painful memory that made Theresa grimace when Roddy was brought into the conversation? Or was there more? And why was Rose covering up about the boy?

That evening she told John Alex, "I've bought a nice little bit of china for Binny's sixtiethth birthday. And guess where I got it?"

"Where?"

"From Rose Fine China on the Danforth."

"Doesn't ring a bell."

"It should. I told you some time ago the Fines have a china and silverware store."

"Ah! right. Seems out of character for Nathan."

"It's a world of surprises, Johnny. Anyway, it's Rose's project. But there's more. Who do I find working there? None other than Theresa Flynn, who's now Mrs. Theresa Bond." John Alex just looked at her across the supper table and only after deliberately buttering a slice of bread did he ask in a quiet way, "And do they have any children?"

"Yes, a boy. That's all I found out and it was Rose that told me. Theresa didn't really want to talk about things. Neither did Rose, really."

"A boy, and just to think..."

"Don't go on Johnny. And anyway, what difference does it make... a boy... a girl..."

"No difference, and you know that isn't what's on my mind. We lost a son and we lost an heir... *that* is the fact."

-1952-

More than the broad moustached face and centre-parted hair, more than the slender-waisted and high-breasted form in white – the feature of the Oldfield's wedding picture that captured the attention was the eyes – bright, discerning, determined.

Jessica held the moulded frame of the picture before her towards the light of the window. On the browning and frayed paper sealing the back she read, *Our Wedding Day, June 25, 1892.* Her mind turned that over. She was born a year later in West Toronto Junction. And a year after that her father started the little works on Siding Street to make springs and axles. What if they had never met, her mother and father, then she would never be. Jimmy would never be. Stop this silliness, she cautioned herself. It was two years ago this very day that Stella's voice shrilled over the phone, "Come quick... quick... Noah's had a fall." She barely took time to cover herself against January. Stella was at the foot of the basement stairs, kneeling beside her husband and gripping his hand. Somehow he had tipped and fallen going down to stoke the furnace. Blood was trickling from his ear.

The funeral went well enough. After all, he was past his

three score and ten – past four score. The rector kept his eulogy short. Throughout the service, Stella sat as ramrod straight as her osteoporosis would allow, discretely dabbing her eyes with an embroidered handkerchief held in her back-gloved hand.

As they filed out of the church behind the coffin, Jessica overheard Shorty Cooper, himself in his eighties, rasping to the younger man supporting him, "A straight shooter, the old man. Built the works up from nothin."

"You can move in with us," Jessica had said, but Stella would have none of it.

When Jessica gently asked, "What about the furnace?" Stella replied, "What about it?"

"I mean shovelling the coal and banking it properly for the night. Why didn't Pappa get oil in? So much easier." "Yes, so much easier. Your father liked coal. That's what he used in iron work. He grew up with coal. There's lots of young boys who will be glad to earn fifty cents shovelling coal twice a day."

"So be it, Momma."

After that, Jessica dropped in on Stella through the week and phoned her religiously at eight every evening. On March 12, 1952, Stella didn't answer the repeated ring. Jessica, John Alex in tow, set out for Annette Street immediately. In the front hall they were met with a wall of coal gas. Between them, they managed to get Stella from where she was slumped in her armchair out to the veranda, but it was too late.

At the funeral service, three days later, as they sang the lines of the final hymn,

Time like an ever flowing stream
Bears all its sons away

200

Jessica whispered to Robina, standing next to her, "and daughters."

★   ★   ★

"How do you like your steak, sir?"

"Medium rare."

"And you, madame?"

"The same."

Years before they would have been celebrating their wedding anniversary at the Walker House, but it had slipped lately, and on this their thirty-fifth anniversary, they were at the Royal York Hotel. "I read somewhere the other day – can't remember who it was – that bonding with a Canadian Anglo is like bonding with a porcupine," said Jessica.

"What's that supposed to mean?" asked John Alex. "I'm an Anglo and you're bonded to me, are you suggesting I'm a porcupine?"

"Not exactly, Johnny, not exactly, but there are times when you are hard to get next to – let us say inscrutable. For instance, where is your mind right now?"

"Hmm."

"See. That's what I mean. You're here, but you're mind is way off somewhere, isn't it?"

"As a matter of fact..."

"It is..."

They had reached the stage when they were not only graying, but also anticipating what the other would say.

"As a matter of fact, I'm thinking of making a will... us making a will."

"The thought has crossed my mind as well."

"The boys at the Board of Trade can't believe that we didn't make one years ago."

"Simple enough. Just a matter of next of kin inheriting. We were looking to Roddy – the bank would finish most of the rest – then the war."

"It's different now."

"Very different."

"I propose we decide on the general direction of things then have a lawyer wrap it up."

"The firm's lawyer?"

"Yes, he's as good as any."

A week later, Terrence Strickland, K.C. said, "About time," when John Alex and Jessica presented him with the will's outline. "I take it you want us to act as your executor." As they nodded their heads, he started to pencil notes furiously.

"On the death of one or the other of the two of you, the entire estate becomes the property of the other. Your collection of photographs and jewellery to Mrs. Russell Dawe."

"Yes."

"And you, J.A., your Military Cross is to go to the Royal Regiment."

"Yes."

"Now, your summer residence, Royal Summer, to be made available for the employees of Royal Spring and Axle. Is that practical?"

"Yes, as a summer camp."

"Oh, yes, and you say here there's to be an endowment out of the residue. Now you want to make certain personal bequests."

"Yes," said Jessica, "and we have them here." He started to read and make notes.

"Ten thousand dollars to each member of the Watt Tyrone family in Humber Bend. Ten thousand dollars to Dan and Amy MacLaren. Ten thousand to Theresa Flynn. Twenty thousand to Doreen Dance, your housekeeper. Is that it? I see you have addresses for all except Theresa Flynn."

"Yes, that's it. We're thinking about the address for Theresa Flynn. For now, just note she is daughter of Maureen Flynn, Shuter Street."

"Uh-huh — try and get me a more specific address. Inheritance becomes a problem without details and a track to follow. Now the residue of your will, what have you on that? Seems to me it's the iceberg, we've just had the tip so far."

"That's so," said John Alex. Jessica pushed another sheet of paper across the desk.

"You're saying here to sell the house on Mohawk Park, all furnishings, cars and the like, cash your bonds and bank accounts, and sell your stock in Royal Spring — you know what that means?"

"Of course."

"Well, there's quite a bit involved here. Can you give me complete details at your convenience. And you say to divide the total residue equally between an endowment for the future Royal Spring and Axle Company camp at Royal Summer and the following: Toronto Diocese of the Anglican Church of Canada, Victoria University, St. Christopher Settlement House, the Toronto Western Hospital and another equal part, unspecified for the present. That's okay, you both look in good health to me. I'll have this ready for you to sign in a couple of weeks. You must feel good about taking this step."

"A damn sight better if we had an heir," growled John Alex.

*   *   *

The rift between Theresa and Addy started over the motorcycle. She was incensed when he came home with it. Out of the blue, so to speak. "Whadda ya think?" he asked. "It's a Harley Davidson. Second hand. Belonged to Martin Sheedy, the old man of that kid who used to pick on Roy."

"That so. And how much did it cost?"

"Two hundred smackers."

"Two hundred! And where did you get that?"

"He's asking twenty-five a month."

"Is he now. Twenty-five a month out of your pay of thirty-five dollars a week. Are you crazy, Addy? And don't let me see Roy on that thing. Understand!"

"You can go to hell, Tess."

She would have attacked him on the spot, but they were on the street standing beside the bike and a few people were starting to gawk attracted by their heated voices.

"Addy's motorcycle is neat," said Roy that evening, scoffing his hot dog supper smothered in catsup. "He says you told him I can't go on it with him. Why not?"

"Why not?" Because those things are dangerous. That's why not."

For the next two weeks, the animus between Addy and Theresa cooled down, but still rankled. When she refused his advances for two nights he shouted at her, "You're a fine damn Catholic." Waking Roy out of his sleep – terrifying him as a row ensued for ten minutes. That Saturday morning, as he pulled on his pants, Addy announced, "I'm going down to Niagara Falls today with some other bikers."

"Go," is all she said. Returning that night after drinking along the way, he and another biker collided. Addy was killed. The other survived with concussion, fractures and lacerations.

Roy wept for days. Addy was the only father he had known. They were close. And Theresa was hit hard, her grief intensified by her guilt that their last days had gone so sour. She never truly loved Addy but she knew he loved her and was fond of Roy.

She took her burden to the confessional and was counselled by the curate to light a candle each day for a month as part of her contrition.

Rose Fine closed the store on the day of the funeral. When Theresa returned to work, Rose said, "There you have it. Jew or gentile, we all have a little time and we're gone. Did Addy have insurance? Don't tell me. I'm putting more in your pay anyway."

"No, Addy didn't have insurance. Never even occurred to him." The pinch was back on Theresa. The pay hike was very welcome.

★   ★   ★

Anita Pucelli — raven-haired, mature beyond her eleven years — was infatuated with Roy. She found him staring through the schoolyard's Frost fence at nothing in particular. "I'm sorry to hear about your father," she said, moving up beside him.

"I don't have a father," he replied, excited by her warm presence.

"Everyone has a father. You mean your father is dead. Everyone knows he died in an accident, but he wasn't a Catholic so he won't go to heaven, will he?"

"That wasn't my father, that was Addy, my stepfather. My real father was killed in the war by the Germans, that's what my mother says."

"Oh, and was your real father a Catholic?" Before he could answer this question for which he had no answer, the bell rang to end recess and Anita, giving him a big smile, said, "See you," and ran off quickly to the girls' entrance.

When Theresa came around that evening after work to collect him at Maureen's, he asked, "Was my real father a Catholic?"

"That's a dumb question," she answered.

"Was he?"

"No he wasn't, but Roddy loved me and that is why you are here."

"Will he be in heaven?"

"I hope so."

"But them that ain't Catholic don't go to heaven?"

"God can work that out."

"What about Addy? He wasn't a Catholic. He did bad things but he did good things too. Where will he go?"

"Really, Roy, your getting on my nerves," she said testily. "How should I know where Addy is anymore than you do? Maybe he's in purgatory where God lets you get ready to go to heaven."

"Oh."

Roy tossed this exchange around in his head before falling asleep. It seemed that his mother's view of the afterlife was a little less open and shut than Father Keogh's, the new curate assisting Father O'Mallery.

The following day, Anita Pucelli waylaid him outside of the drugstore following baseball practice.

"Let's walk together," she said in an adult way.

"Sure."

"I like Father Keogh, don't you?"

"Sure. He's playing me at first base because I have a long reach."

"I don't play sports. Momma needs me at home to help out. Grandma Pucelli helps too. She doesn't speak much English. Do you have a grandma?"

"Sure. Maureen is my grandma. I'm going there now. She speaks English."

"And what about your other grandma? Does she speak English too?"

"My other grandma?"

"Yes, your father's mother. Does she speak English?"

"Oh her. Yeah, sure."

Suddenly, without notice, she pressed against him and kissed him on the cheek. He reddened and bolted away, rounded the corner and flew up the steps to Maureen's flat.

"What's the matter with you boy?" queried Maureen. "Go and wash. I've a jam sandwich for you."

*　　*　　*

Nathan and Rose Fine spent the early part of the Sabbath eve at her parents. The phone was ringing as they came in the door at ten-thirty. "I'll take it," said Rose.

"It's probably Theresa."

"Mrs. Fine?" A brusque male voice inquired. "Mrs. Fine of Rose Fine China?"

"Yes.

"Hatley Jones of the Toronto Evening Telegram."

"So?"

"You haven't heard?"

"Heard what?"

"Mrs. Fine, I hate to be the one to tell you, but your store was robbed an hour and a half ago and the clerk was murdered."

Before he could go on, Rose dropped the receiver to the floor with a bang and shrieked, "My God, my God." As Nathan rushed to put his arm around her, the police were coming to the door to corroborate the unbelievable.

According to a passerby, who phoned the police from a booth across the street from Rose Fine China, the murderers were wearing masks – nylon stockings it emerged later – and ran out of the store to a pick-up truck parked to the east a short way. The police found Theresa's crumpled body behind the open cash register. A small blood splattered crowbar was on the floor in front of the counter. The Evening Telegram reporter and the coroner arrived shortly after the police. Death was instantaneous, the coroner averred, resulting from a blow across the temple by the crowbar.

★   ★   ★

When Robina Dawe picked up the Saturday edition of the Telegram from her veranda, she was on the phone to Jessica Tyrone in a matter of minutes – barely taking time to first grasp some of the front page details:

Danforth Clerk Brutally Murdered
Theresa Bond, 34, will never close the Rose Fine China store again. At nine last evening, as she prepared to leave, two masked assailants marched in on her and ended her life with a crowbar. Police believe her untimely end followed a struggle and estimate about $800 was stolen according to sales slips. Mrs. Bond, a widow, leaves behind her son, Roy 12. See page 8 for diagram and eye-witness account.

Doreen called to Jessica pruning roses in the garden. "Mrs. Dawe on the phone. Says it's urgent."

"Did you see today's paper, Jess?"

"No − hasn't arrived yet − why?"

"Theresa Bond was killed last night in a robbery at the china store... Are you there Jess?"

"Yes, I'm here, Binny. Had to sit down. Go on."

"Everything is here in the paper, Jess. I don't want to go into it over the phone."

"Of course, Binny. I appreciate your call."

"Don't hang up Jess. There's something here I think is news for you."

"Yes."

"The paper says she leaves behind a twelve year old son − Roy."

"Repeat that..."

"She leaves behind a twelve year old son, Roy... Hello, hello, Jess are you still there?"

"Yes, I'm still here Binny."

"You know what this means?"

"It means we've been left in the dark for twelve years."

It was a huge funeral. Rosars had to put on extra staff to

carry flowers from their undertaking parlour to the church. Father O'Malley himself gave the eulogy and celebrated mass. Nathan and Rose Fine sat to the back of the nave with Golda Berman, not far from the Tyrones. "There's the boy with his grandmother Flynn, whispered Golda to Rose, just as Maureen and Roy came past to genuflect before entering their pew.

"So that's Roy. She had him by Roddy Tyrone, the soldier."

"Yeah."

"Handsome."

"Yeah."

At the conclusion of the graveside ritual, the Tyrones headed immediately back to their car. The Fines and Golda were lingering on the road. "This is Golda Berman," Nathan said to Jessica. Rose was dressed in black, looking very strained.

"I've heard about you," Golda said, looking at John Alex. "You have the Royal Spring company. Theresa never told me, but Father O'Malley did, that Theresa's son Roy — his full name is Royal Spring Flynn, did you know? — is your son's child. It always disturbed my late husband, Saul Berman, that Theresa kept Roy a secret from you. She loved your son and his baby. But they weren't married, were they? Maybe that was the reason for the secrecy. I don't know."

"We'll never know," added Rose, gently taking Jessica's hand.

At the church, John Alex had retreated into himself, barely taking in the funeral mass. Where had they gone wrong? How did it happen that they had a grandson who properly should have been a Tyrone, and they didn't even know each other? And what of the boy? What was to become of him without his father or his mother? He twitched on the hard pew, alarming Jessica. Do we have a stake here? We do. We *do*. And he further alarmed Jessica by standing up in his place to look over the heads of Father O'Malley's kneeling parishioners and better see Roy's blond head. Jessica gently pulled at his sleeve. He sat down, and as though it was yesterday and he was shelling garden peas with his mother Joanna in the summer kitchen, her words came back to him, "Your father made his mark and established the mill but you will have an opportunity to do even better and pass on something better still to your children." Suddenly he was touched with a depth of feeling for the boy, his only grandchild, who was a total stranger to him, yet his own flesh and blood.

Now, as Rose held Jessica's hand, he looked across the cemetery at nothing in particular and muttered, "maybe."

"What did you say, dear?" Jessica queried.

"I said 'maybe' – maybe we can enlarge the place of our tent."

"You don't need to speak in riddles, man." said Nathan. "There's a lot you can do for your grandson and now is the time to start."

"It is indeed," said John Alex.